Songbird

DEDICATION

"For my husband, who told me to go chase my dreams.
All my love."

Trigger Warnings:

Verbal and Physical Assault
Kidnapping of a child
Violence
Blood

TABLE OF CONTENTS

CHAPTER ONE
Sage

"Harlow!"

"Dios mío, Harrrrrrrlow!"

Sweet Jesus, where's the fire? I whip my head around trying to find the owner of that voice. Her accent is unmistakable, the way she trills the 'r' in my name carries over the din of the bar. Not immediately seeing her over the bright stage lights, I keep crooning the song despite the very vocal distraction.

It was a busy Saturday night as I sat atop my favorite stool on my favorite stage, in my favorite place; guitar positioned on my lap, singing a Fleetwood Mac cover song. Singing about players loving and playing, I squinted my eyes, trying to scan the crowd for luscious dark hair and curves. Looking over the patrons dancing in front of me, I searched for her.

When I spotted Tess bouncing up and down close to the courtyard entrance, I chuckled into the next lyric. She held her hands high, rolling them in a *'wrap it up'* gesture. Widening my eyes, I shoot her a *'girl give me a minute'* look right back. I'd finish this song then figure out what had her so worked up, I couldn't just stop.

Every once in a blue moon, I'd jump into the lineup. You'd think with a set of pipes like mine, I'd be baring my soul all the time. I'm not trying to toot my own horn, but I'm good, better than good according to some. Do I sing full time though? That's a big fat no. We had bands begging to play here for the most part so I tended to stay in the shadows, only gracing the stage when Tessa's had enough of my hiding.

Three years ago, Tess found this piece of architectural beauty. A little rough around the edges, but it had potential. I still remember the day she charged into my living room and shoved a real estate ad in my face. Disregarding the fact I was in my pajamas; she chucked my pint of ice cream in the trash, threw my house shoes at me and I was dragged along to look with her. She'd always wanted her own bar, and me being me -and let's be honest- Tess being Tess, I let her take me on the ride. In the heart of New Orleans, The Black Cat, was our place. We tackled this just as we've done everything else in the last five years of friendship, together. We're a team, her and I. With a lot of work and a lot more tears, we made it into something amazing.

From the refurbished tables complementing the dark stained floors, to the local artwork and the live bands that played. We took my clean lines and combined her organized chaos to create something truly magnificent. With the 20ft industrial ceilings, the acoustics in here were top notch.

The black stage sits high in the back, surrounded by ambient lighting. Stage lights hanging above in a variety of colors. But I think my favorite part is the rolling garage doors leading to the courtyard. Tessa doesn't have any type of green thumb. She said, 'the closest I'll get to plant life is when I'm packing a pipe'. Her words, not mine. But the courtyard? Ohhh, that was my baby. I took immense pride in the greenery wall, all that wonderful ivy over brick. String lights zig zagging from post to post, surrounding about a dozen tables and comfy couches with open seating. Ferns swaying in the breeze, lavender and mint plants tucked into each corner. It's perfect on a cool evening; we'd light the gas warmers and leave the doors open. Cozy, intimate, but still lively enough that there's a comfort zone for everyone.

This is my home away from home.

Tessa's more "peopley" than I am. "Peopley?", yeah totally the word we're going with. Me, well I'm more Type A, it's not that I don't love people, because I do, how can you work in a bar and not like the general population? I suppose that's the beauty of our arrangement. I don't typically have to deal with the public unless absolutely necessary. Sure, I'll lend a hand when needed. Other than when I'm up here singing my heart out, I hide in the office making sure we have what we need to remain operational, paperwork is my jam, Tessa deals with everything else.

But the music? The easiest explanation for why I'd risk exposing myself is to quote the great philosopher, *Nietzsche, 'Without music, life would be a mistake'.*

Being up on stage is one of the few things that make me feel like *me* again, strumming my guitar and letting my voice be heard, losing myself to the music, each crescendo flowing through me like a river of feeling. It's catharsis at its finest.

Finishing my set, I graciously accepted the applause, feeling energized with a smile on my face. Stepping off the stage, my gaze wanders to where I last saw that lunatic. Catching the tail end of her black hair, I see she's moved on already, never idle. Gliding to the bar, I watch as she takes a moment to talk to one of the new bartenders, when she sees me headed in her direction, she walks through the back, and I know she's going to our shared office.

Tess opens the door for us letting me breeze by first, closing it behind her. I grab a water bottle out of the mini fridge and before I can even bring it to my lips, she's on me.

"Mami, if I am hollering for you, then you oughta know it's

serious." She eyes me, hands on her hips, toe tapping with impatience.

"Consider me especially scolded. Noted from this point forward." I fall dramatically onto the leather sofa.

"Now that you're good and chastised. I was trying to get your attention because April called."

"Jericho okay?" I ask sitting upright, immediately worried.

She answers me on a sigh, "Yes, everything's fine, but Jeri is throwing up. Said she wouldn't have even bothered you, but it hasn't stopped after the first couple times."

I nod my head, "Okay, yeah. You've got this right?" I ask, already gathering my purse.

She scoffs, "Have I got this? Mami. We're fine. I've got enough servers tonight, it's handled. Send the teenager packing and give mi niña some love."

"Will do, love you T." I call over my shoulder as I rush out of the office.

I hear her call out from behind me. "Sí, mamá, yo también te amo!"

It takes me about 20 minutes to get home. It's not too late, I'd already been planning to be home before 10pm. With April calling, I'm home at least an hour earlier than that.

Pulling into my driveway, I glance at my overgrown yard with a groan; I really need to mow. We've just moved in last week. After the last year in an apartment building, I should be glad we *even have the damn yard*; I need to remember that and do the work. *Silver linings am I right?* I trudge up my porch and let myself into the house. April is sitting on the sofa, looking absolutely drained.

Setting my keys in the entryway dish and hanging my purse on the hook, I addressed her with a grimace. "You doing okay, where's Jeri?"

I'm sure she figured this would be an easy gig. Not many 16-year-olds know how to handle a pukey situation, but since there's no mess in my living room and my kitchen looks clean, I think she's done exceptionally. Faint traces of Lysol in the air tell me she cleaned up shortly before my arrival. As I look around appreciatively, she rises from her position on the sofa and moves toward the front door.

"Yeah, I'm good. Dead on my feet but I was more worried about Jeri, she's sound asleep by the way. Sorry to bother you, but I was kind of panicking. Homegirl went down after I called."

"No worries, I'd rather you reach out if you need to. Did it just start out of nowhere?"

She winces, "Well, I think it may have been partially my fault."

Sitting on the arm of the sofa she just vacated, I ask, "How so?"

Wringing her hands, she says, "I let her have ice cream tonight after we left the arcade, not realizing she'd already had a slice of choco-chunk pizza. I think it may have been sweets overload."

Quirking a brow, I ask, "She got that one by you, did she?"

She laughs nervously, "Yeah, she totally did. She finally admitted it as I was cleaning chocolatey pieces out of her hair."

"Oh no." I cover my mouth, trying to withhold the giggle bubbling up.

"Oh yes, she's something all right. She gave me those big puppy dog eyes and talked me into going through the creamery." April shakes her head as she continues gathering her things.

"She should be good by tomorrow if that's the case." Maneuvering to my purse, "Here, let me pay you. Also, is your dad still up to taking her to camp?" Jericho's been going off the rails with excitement all summer. We've counted down the days until soccer camp. Fortunately, and maybe unfortunately, Brad's the coach. April and June's (*yes, like the months of the year*) dad is a super sweet guy. In the last year of knowing each other, he's shown interest several times. *Unfortunately for him*, I shut that down gently when he finally plucked the courage to ask me out. I'm not looking. Not now, maybe not ever. Luckily, because he is so nice, he agreed to settle for friendship, and we were able to move past it. Which works better for me because Jeri and June are besties, and now that we're neighbors, I'd like smooth sailing.

"Yeah, as long as she's feeling okay tomorrow afternoon. We're all set to go. June's been driving dad up the wall. We went to the arcade with them earlier and the girls were in full soccer mode. Dad had to tell them the basketball game was *not for feet*." She shakes her head in exasperation.

"Those girls. I swear."

"Well Miss H, I'd better get home." She hooks a thumb over her shoulder, gesturing for the front door.

Grabbing $50 out of my wallet I walk her to the porch and watch as she treks the two houses to her own. Once I see she's safely inside, I arm the security system before peeking at Jeri in bed and hitting the shower.

As I wash my hair, I think about all the things I still need to do. I took the next five days off so I could finish getting us settled while Jericho is gone. As a friend, Brad put in a good word with the homeowner, and we were able to move into this neighborhood from an apartment complex across town. It's quieter, *which I love*. It has a private fenced back yard and small patio area, which Jeri and I *both love*. Just two bedrooms, but instead of the one bathroom we previously shared, I have my own ensuite and there's a full guest bathroom in the hall. The open floor plan leads into a gallery style kitchen and dining nook. I love the hardwood floors and soft neutral colors encompassing each room, I won't change a thing. It's perfect for us.

After I towel off, I throw on a pair of cotton panties and an old t-shirt, the neckline is frayed and the material has gotten thin, but I refuse to get rid of it no matter how often Tessa tells me I need to. The comfort I get when I wear this shirt means more to me than I can put into words. Heading down the hallway, I opened Jeri's door quietly. Trying not to disturb her sleeping form, I crept to her bed and laid a hand on her forehead. No fever, that's good. She seems to be snoozing peacefully. Pulling the baby monitor from a box in her room, I set it up on the floor beside her bed and turned it on. You'd think once your child reaches the age of seven, the monitor wouldn't be necessary. But that's a load of horseshit. This little baby has lasted us this long and it comes in handy on nights like this. I can hear the first signs of vomiting and race in to save my floors, or the bed.

Running my fingers through soft curls, I admire her delicate features and the smattering of freckles that match my own. If she were to open those beautiful eyes, she'd be the spitting image of her father. From the blue-black hair to her molten silver irises. Every day is a reminder of what we're missing. Looking at her, I'm filled with both love and longing. Leaning down, I press a soft kiss to her forehead before heading back to my room.

In bed I'm restless, after spending the better part of an hour staring at my ceiling, I release a frustrated breath before flinging myself over and digging the burner cell from my bedside drawer. It takes just a minute for it to power up as I lay there anxiously chewing my thumb nail, waiting for any new notifications. This is my nightly ritual; one I'd love to do away with all together. The ever present thought, 'what if', isn't a good time.

10/10 do not recommend.

It keeps me in a near constant state of paranoia. Finally, after what seems like an eternity, my brother's name pops up. Just one text.

Thorne: Still safe.

I replied.

Sage: Good looking out.

My heart rate eases, and I power the phone down before placing it back in my drawer, before too long, I feel myself drifting to sleep.

I'm running, mama is screaming for me to keep going, so I do. This hallway is so long. There's glass on the floor. My feet are bleeding, and my throat hurts from the smoke. I keep running, I can hear mama behind me. I slip on something. Mama grabs me by the arm and hauls me with her. I don't know how she's moving so fast. Her big belly is bouncing with every hard step we take. "We have to get to the safe house. We have to get to the safe house." She mutters as we move. I slipped again. This time someone else grabs me, I start to fight. Mama tells me to stop, he's a friend. 'We have to keep going.' The scene fades, I'm in a car now. Huddled in the back seat. We've been driving forever and I'm hungry. My feet hurt. I pull the blanket off my toes so I can see. I remember now, I stepped in the glass. Mama must have bandaged me when I was sleeping because I can see their white wrappings, little dots of blood peek through. Looking at the front, I can see mama whispering to someone. The man who picked me up. He's driving, gripping the wheel so tightly his hands look white. They're trying to be quiet, but I can make out mama saying, "He can never find her." She looks back at me, she's crying, with one hand on her belly, she runs the other through my hair. "Mo chroí. Go back to sleep." I close my eyes. Something wakes me, but I can't open my eyes, it's dark. I'm trapped. I can't breathe. I can hear my mama's voice. She's scared.

"Mo chroí, time to wake up."

"Wake up Sage."

"Sage, wake up!"

Waking with a gasp, I jackknife in bed, kicking at the sheets wrapped around my legs, I pause, getting my bearings with a hand clasped to my chest. There's no air in the room, no air in my lungs. With several deep inhales, I take in my surroundings. A sliver of moonlight coming in through my curtains highlights the familiar space. I'm home. It's safe. Slowly, I start my breathing techniques, trying to abate the panic attack and repeat my rehearsed mantra to my empty room.

"We are safe."

"They don't know where we are."

"Jericho is safe."

"We're alive."

Just saying the words out loud helps. After a few more deep breaths, I'm feeling marginally calmer. Glancing at the clock on my nightstand, the red numbers show it's a quarter to six. I could get a little more sleep, or I could work off this excess adrenaline. Choosing the latter, I clamber from bed and throw on gym shorts and a sports bra. Grabbing a protein bar and bottle of water from my kitchen, I clasp my smart watch around my wrist and walk into the garage. It's still mild, the excessive New Orleans heat not hitting this early. After cracking the garage door about a foot, I leaned into my stretch. Hitting my calves, quads and hamstrings while I roll my neck a few times, hoping to shake away the nightmare's residue. In a brisk walk, I eat the protein bar and drink a few sips of water before cranking up the intensity.

One foot in front of the other, running harder and harder until there are no thoughts, only the next step. Losing myself in the rhythm, feeling the burn in my lungs, I'm flying. My feet pound against the black rubber belt. Sweat pours down my back and my traitorous thoughts shut down. Slowly drifting from myself. Each step is a tune only I can hear, the thumping rhythm is its own sort of music. If I can't sing, this is the next best thing. As my feet glide over the stationary track, there are no worries, no fears. My brain is base instinct, telling me one thing. 'Keep going.'

I run for what feels like forever before I hear slipper covered feet shuffling towards me. She's trying to be quiet, but her presence is undeniable. Like a storm cloud rolling in, I can feel the charge in the air. Sweat dripping down my chest and back, I don't stop while looking for Jericho out of the corner of my eye. She likes to play these games. Not happening today ma'am. Grinning to myself, I pretend not to notice and wait.

When she gets close enough to touch, I call out "Ahhhh!" She shrieks and I laugh.

"Mom! Not fair! You knew I was here!" She has her hands pressed dramatically to her chest, small lungs heaving. Slowing my pace, I'm walking instead of the full out sprint I'd been doing, trying to cool down before stopping completely.

Jeri comes around so she's in my line of sight. She's practically giddied this morning. Bouncing from foot to foot.

"You move like a herd of elephants miss thing. What's got you so excited?" I already know, but I love to tease.

"We've got to get ready to go mom, Coach Brad said we leave at 12." She hops up and down while holding the front of my treadmill, I glance down at my watch and look back at her with wide eyes.

"Girl, it's only 8am. We've still got four hours before you leave. Are you trying to run off on me early?"

"No, I'd never run off," she rolls her eyes, "but I'm ready to goooo." She stamps a small foot and whines.

Arching a brow, I eye her critically, "How are you feeling? How's the tummy?"

"I'm fine. Promise." Holding a pinky out to me, I wrap mine around hers and watch as she brings both our hands to her lips in a quick kiss before giving me a cheeky grin, all dimples.

"Uh huh, well how about this? You go change out of those

cutie patootie pajamas, and I'll go freshen up. Then we'll grab breakfast with Tia Tess?"

Eyes growing with excitement, she squeals, "We'll go to Beignet Barn?"

"Sure, if that's what you want?"

"YES!" She fist pumps in the air and scurries off to throw on God knows what.

I'm left to cool down, with a smile on my face and a lightness in my soul.

After a quick shower, I threw on a white crop top over a lace bralette and cut off denim shorts. I'm slipping on my sandals when Jeri struts out of her bedroom. It's hard not to laugh, but I suppress it. She's taken to picking out her own clothes, it's a battle I'm not going to fight. At seven, I'm encouraging independence. She's got on cheetah print bike shorts, a hot pink oversized Led Zepplin tee that reaches almost to the hem of her shorts -*fairly sure that one is mine but whatever*- a bright orange crossbody and teal blue Chuck Taylor's. Looking at me expectantly, I don't rain on her parade, asking, "You ready rockstar?"

Instead of a verbal response, she grabs a pair of my sunglasses off the entry table and waves her hand saucily in a 'let's go' motion before bounding down the steps and hopping into my truck. *Oh, this girl.* She's a storm of black curls and sass. I stand there stunned for a moment before rolling my eyes and following.

Let's be real, wherever she goes, I'll always follow.

When we pull into Beignet Barn, Tess is already seated. She sees Jeri come through the doors and waves us over enthusiastically. Before I can reach the booth, Tess has her wrapped up in a crushing hug.

"Sí, niña!" She holds her at arm's length to look at her before rapid firing in Spanish. "Te ves increíble chica bonita!"

This is typical, they'll have a whole ass conversation as if I'm not here. Claiming my seat across from them in the plush booth, they continue. "Muchas gracias Tia Tessa." Jeri smiles bashfully, twisting side to side.

Tessa side eyes her before asking slowly, so Jeri can pick up out the words. "¿Te vististe tú mismo?" After a moment, Jeri bites her lip and looks at me, I just shrug, feigning ignorance and nod encouragingly for her to answer.

"Sí, mamá dijo que podía ponerme lo que quisiera." She grins widely, all teeth and dimples. When she responds with no mistakes, Tessa laughs aloud and hugs her again.

"Oh, niña you're doing so well! We'll have you speaking fluently in no time! I'm so proud of you." Jericho scampers into the booth beside her. The server brings me a coffee and some breakfast for Jeri, I thank her and then thank Tess for ordering ahead. I'm absolutely starving this morning after my longer than normal run.

I've just taken a healthy sip of my latte when Tessa finally addresses me, it's like she waits for the most opportune moment to ruffle my feathers.

"So, I was wondering if I could steal her for a bit this morning?"

"Oh, you noticed I'm here after all?" I ask dryly.

She doesn't respond to my snark, just looks at me coyishly, batting her lashes. Jeri looks ready to burst with excitement, she bites down on her lip looking between the two of us. I know what she'd rather do.

With a pout I reply, "But I'm already not going to see her for a week."

Jeri goes to answer, but Tess stops her and whispers in her ear. They have a quiet conversation before nodding at each other in unison and returning their attention back to me.

"It's not really a week mom, only five days, how about this?"

"Oh, we're bargaining?" I ask, brow raised, stifling a smile.

"Don't interrupt mom, it's rude." She looks at Tess like *'can you believe her'*, Tessa nods sympathetically. Zipping my lip with a flourish, I stay quiet until she continues.

"How about, Tia Tess takes me for just a little bit, so we can get our nails done," she takes a bite of her beignet, talking as she chews, "and then," She glances at Tess who nods for her to keep going, "you can take me to lunch before we meet coach Brad? That's called compromise mom."

I pretend to mull it over, "Compromise? That's a big word for a seven-year-old." I lift my latte with both hands, giving Tess an admonishing look over the rim of my cup as I take a sip

"Not too big if I can use it." She says matter of factly before taking another bite, Tessa cackles at that. I suppose she's got me there.

Holding up a finger I ask, "May I speak?" She considers while chewing and then nods. "I agree to those terms." She hops from her seat and does a 'floss' as Tess and I watch on, giggling at her antics.

A morning with my girls was much needed. After the nightmare woke me, my anxiety was at an all-time high. Distracted by the fresh goodies being put out, Jericho runs over to the bakery display giving me and Tess a moment to ourselves. Swiveling around in the booth, I kick my feet up on the empty space, not taking my gaze off my girl. I watch as she presses her face to the glass case.

Without turning, I ask Tess, "You'll look after her?"

Tessa sets her coffee down. "I won't let her out of my sight."

Lowering my voice down to a whisper, "Thorne text me last night."

She asks just as quietly, "What did yummy big brother have to say?"

"Firstly, never refer to my brother as 'yummy' in a conversation with me, we've gone over this. It's just gross. Secondly, he said the same thing he's said the last four years, 'still safe'. We're good, for now."

I peek at her in my periphery. Her head canted, looking thoughtful.

"What is it?" I asked, turning to her fully.

She chews on the corner of her mouth, glancing over at Jeri before bringing her eyes back to mine. "Are you sure you want to send her to camp this year?"

The answer to that is something I've stewed over for weeks. I blew a small raspberry, rolling my lips, gaze moving back to Jeri. "She deserves every opportunity to be a kid. I held her back last summer. It isn't fair. You tell me all the time to start living. How can I keep her hidden too? They're not looking for her, they're looking for me."

Before we get too dark; she asks with a serpent's smile. "So, what are you going to do with yourself for five whole days?" I can hear the light tease in her tone. Rolling my neck in her direction, narrow my eyes, even though I'm grateful for the change in subject. Dark lashes bat playfully over caramel eyes. She's giving me her best innocent face, but that's bullshit, and we both know it.

Holding up my hand, I start ticking items off my fingers one by one. "Oh, you know, mow my grass. Organize our house, put things away, probably come into work and-"

"Get some dick." She cuts in.

"Tessalynn Sanchez." I admonish sternly.

"What?"

"Could you be any louder?" I whisper harshly, "I'm not looking to get any dick."

"I could be louder, is that a challenge?" My face floods with embarrassment and she ignores it, "Kitty cat then? I'm mean whatever floats your boat hermana."

I choke on a laugh. "No, not that either."

She sighs dramatically, "Harlow, I love you. But I feel bad for your poor unused vagina. I can hear it weeping every day. 'Fill me, somebody filllll meeee'." She sounds like a Latina ghost auditioning for the part at a haunted house.

Denial isn't just a river in Egypt.

The blush working up my neck and chest betrays me. "My vagina isn't unused. Clearly, I have a child." I say gesturing to said seven-year-old, who's currently salivating over the chocolate croissants.

"Clearly." She deadpans.

"It's a choice. I don't have time to be dicked down, Tessie. It would only bring more complications in my already complicated life."

Rolling her eyes, she asks, "Don't you think you could use a reprieve from all the stress?"

"Probably, but it's not going to happen."

"Let me ask this, when is the last time someone went down there to change your oil?" She waves her fingers, eyeing my shorts in reiteration. "You've had offers, and you always shut them down. Sorry to tell you, but it needs to be said, you creak like the *Tin Man* when you walk. It's getting out of hand. You don't need to form an attachment; you just need a good fuck."

I stared at her, absolutely dumbfounded. "I don't have an answer for that."

"At this point, I'm sure you could invest stock in any battery company you wanted, you need to get back in the saddle." When I start to contradict her, she holds up a hand silencing me, "I do know a particular Coach that's been dying to service you in that department. He even helped you move closer to him, el amor de Dios Harlow. One of these days, that poor organ is just going to shrivel up and die!"

"I'm not sleeping with Brad. Like I said, it's a complication I don't need." I whispered harshly; arms crossed defensively; I turned back to watch Jeri. Naturally, Tessa's not finished.

"You miss him, don't you?" The question is a gut punch, and she knows it. Emotion starts tightening my throat.

"Lo siento. I shouldn't have asked."

I answer anyway, "Every damn day." It comes out a rasped whisper.

We finish breakfast and Jeri gives me a full body hug before Tess leans in to do the same. She whispers in my ear, "You're not a true ghost, cariño. Don't let this really kill you."

It's not a guarantee I can make. This is the longest we've been in one place. Thorne would let me know if there was even an inkling of danger on our doorstep. Maybe Tessa's right. Maybe I should live a little. I can't go back to my old life. I can't go back to Jeri's dad. Even though most days, every single fiber in my body screams for him.

When you fake your death, there's no going back to before.

CHAPTER TWO

Dean
Ravens MC Clubhouse
48 hours Prior

"Yo Dean!", my father bellows across the bar, I pop my head up quickly at his summons. The way he's looking at me, this is serious. Angus Graham is rarely, if ever upset. Right now, though, the calm he usually exudes is nowhere to be found. He shoots me a 'come-hither' motion with his hand and points toward the hallway leading to his office. My brother and I share a look, and I nod my head towards the keg I was tapping.

"Donnie, take this over, will you?", he slides in to take my place and gestures for me to hop to it. We don't like to keep dad waiting. Dusting my hands off my well-worn jeans, I take a deep breath and trudge across the clubhouse bar room.

Man, what I wouldn't give for a cold beer right now, I got off the road earlier than expected, all I wanted was a cold beer, a good meal and to sleep. Apparently Pops has a different idea.

Several heads turn, but no one makes direct eye contact with me, strange, but okay. What do they know that I don't? I just got back from a Florida run, meeting with a new weapons distributor. Haven't even been in the clubhouse 30 minutes and now this?

What the fuck have my brothers done?

Walking into dad's office I see he's already sitting at his large barnwood desk, tattooed arms crossed over his barrel chest. He motions me to close his door before I go to take a seat. Backtracking, I close the door and rather than sit, I stand. I'm familiar with this office, I grew up here. Being the Vice President of the Raven MC means many a meeting with dear old dad across from his desk. Brainstorming and planning, or occasionally just spending time together, especially after mom passed.

Being the eldest of his three sons, I bear the most responsibility and let's be honest, I'm the club fixer. I can only imagine what this meeting entails. Thinking back to the last few weeks and coming up with nothing.

My younger brother Donal, or Donnie as we call him, has been keeping me up to speed as our Master of Arms. To my knowledge, we haven't had a problem with the last few runs. The surrounding MCs haven't given us any issues in years. Our baby brother Knox has been keeping up with our earnings as our Treasurer. No problems come to mind, most of our earnings are legit these days and he's not called anyone else in with us. Plus, Knox is in Texas visiting another charter, cleaning their books. He's been there several months, getting an 'in' with the Cartel.

As I said, strange. Glancing around the room, I take in the deep blue walls that I know like the back of my hand. There's the portrait of my mother, Bea, hung behind my dad's back, so she can watch over all of us. Then there's the photos of us through the years. Mismatched frames scattered around. An older one stands out, Donnie's graduation. Trying my best to avoid the copper head of hair next to me, I focus on my brothers faces. Knox stands between us, both arms slung around my and Don's shoulders, grinning that dimpled smile. My brothers have the same silver eyes and black hair, the eyes we inherited from our father, the hair... that was our mother. Pops used to call her Snow; he'd say she was his own personal princess, and she called him Grumpy, much to his amusement.

Finally pulling my attention back to the big man in front of me, the energy feels different, charged. He's still strong, always has been, but I can see tension in his shoulders and the line of his jaw is tight. He still fills out the black henley he wears under his Raven MC cut, his 1% and Presidents Patch distressed from years of riding and fighting. But there's red in the whites of his silver eyes, like he hasn't been sleeping. Whatever he's going to drop on me, it can't be good.

Nervous energy radiates from him in waves. The few times my father called me in here looking like this, it didn't end well. First it was to let my brothers and I know mom had cancer. Six months after that, it was to plan her funeral, another year after that, it was to let me know my girl was gone.

It's been eight years.

The desk he's sitting at is a replacement after I broke the old one in a fit of rage. Every time I see it, it's a reminder. Shutting my eyes, I give myself a pep talk.

Fuck don't go there Dean. Just. Don't. You can't change the past.

Needing a distraction, I run my fingers through my black hair, it's gotten long, the curled ends hanging just below my shoulders. Surprisingly, I don't mind it.

Pulling the elastic off my wrist, I tie it back into a bun just to give my hands something to do. My fingers are my only tell, when I'm stressed, or nervous. I find my fingers itching to move. Dad still hasn't said a word, this must be bad. He stares at me; I can see him stewing. There's a frown on his brow and his lips are pressed into a tight line, for the life of me, I can't figure out what's wrong.

Fucking finally, he breaks the silence, leaning forward on his elbows with a smirk, "You're growing out the beard now too?"

My fingers rub across the growth, I didn't intend for it to get this long either, but now that it has, I've got to admit, I like it too. Especially when I pull my baclava across my face before a ride, the beard helps keep it where it belongs.

"Why not? I don't mind it Pop."

He's still dancing around something. He's not one for small talk, the thing about my father, he speaks with a purpose. Whatever this is, it really can't be good.

"Have a seat Aberdean."

Fuck, he never calls me Aberdean. I can't sit. Instead, I stand there and wait.

"Pop, whatever it is, just tell me. Rip the band aid-" The end of that sentence is left hanging when dad interrupts me.

"We've got trouble brewing again."

This is serious.

"What kind of trouble?"

He growls through his teeth, so low I almost didn't catch it, "The same trouble that was brewing eight years ago."

"The Russians?" He nods.

I press on, my pulse quickening. "They're brewing trouble here?"

He nods again. I'm starting to lose my patience.

"Pop's I'm going to need you to elaborate. It's been a long fucking day."

Easing back in his chair, he brings a hand up to rub his temples. I'll give him just a moment to gather his thoughts. True to form, he does.

"The Russians have been systematically visiting charters from Vegas to Louisiana. They were around while you were gone, but they've moved off. Last I heard, they've made it to New Orleans.

We've dealt with the Russians before. You know this. McGregor wants us to keep an eye on them. Figure out what they're doing. The Saints MC down in NOLA asked if you'd come down while they're visiting. I'm sure you remember Pete Jr, well, his old man died a couple weeks ago, passed the torch. He could use a friendly face while the Bratva is in the area. The Saints' new Prez asked for my fixer. That's you Aberdean."

"Did they cause any trouble while they were here?" I ask, my mind running a mile a minute.

"No, that was part of what has me concerned. One of the guys mentioned they paid a visit to Hattie Mason."

That gets a rise out of me. "What did Thorne have to say about that?"

"They're still not speaking. Haven't been for years. Shortly after the reported visit, she hopped on a bus to Texas. We assumed she was going to visit Fern, he called her. She said if Hattie shows up, she'll let him know. How that woman raised two good kids, I'll never know."

"So, they're gone now?" I rub my fingers across my temple, trying to ease the oncoming headache.

"Seem to be, but I'm not going to get complacent. The Bratva numbers have grown in the last ten years, Colin thinks they're gearing up to take him on again, but it's like they're waiting for something. We're on guard until we have more details."

I groan, "I just got back from Florida Pop's. This would have been nice to know before I got all the way back here. How soon do I need to go?"

"Tomorrow." He smirks at me, "I could've told you sooner had I'd known you were coming home early. You should have called." Fuck. He's got me there. I didn't want to tell him because I wanted a few extra days at home. Lot of good that did me.

Honestly, I understand the urgency. We're in McGregor's territory, running his guns and other contraband. He and my father have always been friends, especially after he helped him decades ago. An insurgence was started by one of his men, leading to the disappearance of McGregor's pregnant wife and the death of his child during the fire that destroyed his estate. In the aftermath, my father helped smuggle an injured Colin McGregor to safety. Our MC nursed him back to health, then aided him in ridding the traitors and dealing with the Russians who were backing them. After days of torture, where I hear Colin unleashed hell on Vasiliy Medvedev, he displayed his broken body for the remaining members of the Medvedev bratva. A statement had to be made.

You don't fuck with the Irish.

Against Colin's order, my father pulled the trigger, ending the last Pakhans reign. Colin was losing himself in the madness and my father put a stop to it. Vasily along with the others responsible were put down that day. It was a bloody time. I don't remember much; I was just a kid. But I do remember the fear on my mother's face and how she held us a little tighter.

Pulling myself from those thoughts, I agree to what he's asking. "Alright, give me tonight, Pop's. I'll ride out tomorrow, but I'm taking Donnie with me."

He nods in approval. "Yeah, his ass could use a run. Keep him on his toes Dean." He dismisses me with a wave of his hand. Somebody's got to break the news to Donnie, I'm relishing the fact it's me. If my night's getting ruined, so should his.

Walking back into the bar, my brother looks at me, brows furrowed in suspicion at the slight smile on my face. Sliding me a tumbler of whiskey, we don't say a word to each other and I down it in one go. When I continue to stand there and smile at him, he starts fidgeting.

"You going to keep in suspense all day or tell me what he wanted?" He eyes me sardonically.

"We're going on a trip little brother." I clap him on the shoulder, shaking him, before brushing past and grabbing a pint glass off the back wall. I fill it to the brim from the keg I was tapping earlier and settle into one of the armchairs across from the pool tables.

Like I knew he would, Donnie makes his way to where I'm sitting and plops his ass on the coffee table directly in front of me. Blocking my view of the room.

"Where are we going?"

"That tables not going to hold your weight."

Rolling his eyes, he ignores me. "Where are we going?"

I drew circles in the condensation on my glass while answering him. "NOLA."

"What's in New Orleans?"

Trying to answer his own question, the wheels turn in his brain, but they're too slow for me. With an eyeroll of my own I put him out of his misery. "We're going there to back up Petey Brandt. His dad died, so he's Prez now. Word is he's got company in town and could use extra eyes at his back."

Huffing dramatically, Donnie crosses his arms over his chest. "The man's got an entire clubhouse full of brothers for that. Why do we need to go?"

When I just shrug, Donnie narrows his eye and his lips pull down.

"Don, don't act like a petulant child, you're a 26-year-old man. Pops said we're needed, so we're going."

"Well, I don't want to go."

I laugh loudly. When he huffs again, I laugh even louder. He looks so smug sitting there on that little table. It's quite the picture. This pouting grizzly of a man, it's comical.

Wiping the tears from my eyes, I try to sober up. The reason for the visit is a serious, and he needs to understand that. "Don.

I wouldn't have asked for you to come with me if it wasn't important. I can't explain now, but I will when we're alone. Besides, what are you going to do here? Aren't you bored?"

He throws his hands up, "Of course I'm fucking bored. I never said I wouldn't go," he grumbles, "just that I didn't want to go there. For fucks sake, it's not even Mardi Gras. Where's the fun in that?"

Shaking my head at his fatuous display, I grin. "Donnie, when haven't we made our own fun?"

He considers this before slapping both hands on his knees and rising. As he walks away, he calls over his shoulder, "Fair enough."

Now that I'm alone, I can take a minute to view my surroundings. Music is playing somewhere but I'm not really hearing it. Trying to shut off my mind for a bit, I drain almost all of my beer in two gulps. Letting my eyes wander for a minute, I watch a few of the guys in the middle of a pool game, then move on to observe some old timers playing poker at one of the tables.

"When do we leave?" Donnie asks from his position at the bar.

With one last gulp, I polish off the last of my beer before setting the glass down beside me. "6am."

He nods sharply and salutes lazily before sauntering off towards the girls in the kitchen. I don't blame him for seeking out some relief before we leave, there's no telling what we're walking into on this run. Me though? I'm not interested. I've had the same girl on my mind for years. I don't want anyone else, and I can't bring myself to betray her memory.

Leaning back in the armchair, I take a moment to appreciate the space. Some things never change. The sweet butts are off in the kitchen area, putting toppings on a pizza. A group of my MC brothers sit on the stools and make requests. I'm glad their days aren't going to shit.

Home sweet home.

Chuckling quietly at my own sarcasm, a few of the girls notice me and shoot soft smiles. They know I'm not interested in what they have to offer, but I'm at least polite, I return their smiles with a small one of my own.

That's when I notice Vicki headed out of the kitchen, wearing sky-high heels and a fucking Daisy duke bikini top, little hot pants with her ass half out. I don't see the appeal. But my little brother Knox goes bananas for the shit she puts down. When she sees me, her eyes light up and she beelines in my direction. Without a care for my personal space, she boldly drapes herself over the back of my chair.

Fuck not this again.

Maybe if I'm quiet, she'll just go away.

If I pretend I don't see her, maybe she'll disappear.

"What's the matter Dean, you okay baby?", her voice is grating. She should know better by now, rolling my eyes, I look at her over my shoulder, "Vicki, you need to back off." It's a rumble bubbling from my chest.

"Vick, don't." Donnie calls across the room.

"Mind your business, Donal." She snaps back.

"Vick, darlin', you're barking up the wrong tree today. Don't say I didn't warn you." My brother laughs sardonically.

Don't lose control, don't lose control. She's not worth it.

I repeat the mantra in my head, hoping that I can take my own advice.

"Dean, I could make you feel so good, just give me a chance." She whispers in my ear before throwing her long brown locks over one shoulder and pressing closer. Blatantly ignoring Donnie's warning. Objectively, Vicki is a decent-looking woman, but she's not the one I want. She's all I see when I close my eyes.

My Songbird.

With her copper hair and sky-blue eyes, the freckles that ran along the bridge of her nose and cheeks like my very own constellations. When I close my eyes, I still smell the lemongrass scent that trailed wherever she went. Every night spent kissing her under the willow tree and sneaking her into the clubhouse, into my bed. I've loved Sage since I was 13 years old, she was it for me. There's a hollow cavity in my chest, when she died, my heart burned with her.

"Vicki, I need to you to get off me, I'm not Knox." but she doesn't, in fact she creeps her hands further down my chest, on a collision course with my belt. Blatantly ignoring my request. As her hands drift further, I grab her wrists quickly, stopping the movement and she sucks in a sharp breath. There's excitement in her dark eyes, but this isn't going to go the way she's hoping it will. With a smirk, I leaned in close, watching as her pupils dilated with need. Abruptly, I burst her bubble, twisting our positions and dumping her unceremoniously into my vacated seat. I'm up and striding away before she has time to plant herself back in front of me.

"I've told you, you're better off playing with someone else." Donnie chuckles from across the room.

I'm still trying to maintain a level of decency. It's the same song and dance with her every time. Always trying to push herself on me and I'm always pushing her off. If my brother didn't enjoy her company so much, I'd have told her to leave the club. The woman's like a dog in heat, hounding and sniffing around me whenever I'm here. I'm not interested in making her or any of the other girls here my old lady. I already had one of those, she died.

"Why are you still pining over a ghost? It's letting other opportunities for happiness pass you by. She's dead." Each word is a barb. Stopping me in my tracks. The club descends into silence. I see Donnie moving closer to me from my peripheral.

"She was trash, she'd always been trash. I don't understand what she had-"

Before anyone can stop me, I've taken four steps back and pulled my gun from behind my back. I'm not aiming at her, but the intent is clear.

Is it extreme? Yes.

Do I care? No.

Am I really going to shoot her? Pfft.....

Scare her? Definitely.

Her face is ashen and there are sweat beads on her overly inflated upper lip. I know I look insane, baring my teeth in a savage grin, daring her to open her mouth. Challenging her to say something else. If this is the measure I need to take for her to understand the status quo, then I suppose it'll have to do. I'm not sure if the woman knows what the word 'no' means, but from now on, she won't have the opportunity.

In a menacing growl, I answer her ridiculous question. "You want to know what she had? My soul Vick, that girl had my soul. So, if you're asking if I still have one to show mercy for the disrespect, the answer is no. Do you see this?" I gesture to the tattoo in the center of my neck. It's a raven, wings spread for flight, clutching a bundle of sage in its talons. Under that, it reads 'Songbird'. "She may not have borne my mark Vick, but I carry hers."

Before I know what's happing, her eyes roll back into her skull as she passes out.

Not quite what I was going for, but whatever works. "Huh, would you look at that."

I need to go before she comes to, *and I actually shoot her.*

Turning to leave, Donnie hollers at me, "Do you want company?"

"Nope, I'll see you in the morning. Don't be late Don. Also, you need to be the one to tell Knox she's gone. I fucking mean it too.

I want her off club property within the hour. Give her some cash to find a place to stay, but she won't be back. I'll call you later man." I head out front where my bike is parked.

I need to get out of here.

Hopping on my bike, I fire it up and head to my house a few miles down the way. The plan is to wash this day off me, eat, sleep, in that order. I won't make it without proper rest. I learned the hard way not to push my body to those extremes. The first two years after Sage's death were the worst. Insomnia became my normal and booze my solution. A lot of people got hurt, I did the hurting. The path I traveled got darker and darker. Jora, my best friend -and club lawyer-, along with Thorne -Sage's brother of all people- were the ones who got my head on straight. Jora advocated on my behalf and Pops started sending me on longer runs, far away from here, the distance helped.

With the wind on my face, the freedom of the road and the vibrations of my Harley, I take my first full breath since meeting with my old man. Taking the long way home, I loop through town. I don't plan to stay on my bike forever, just long enough to empty my head, so far, it's not working. That's part of my problem. I never feel peace anymore, especially in Ravenswood. There's a creature in my chest, scraping his claws across my ribs, waiting to break free from the prison I've pushed him into. A darkness in my soul that leaves me deeply unsettled. It's a daily battle to remain in control. I haven't felt content in years and the clubhouse no longer feels like home. I've only recently started admitting it to myself, during my last run, I wanted to come back early, take a few days and see if the resentment still festered.

Truthfully, I know it would have.

After opening my garage, I park my bike and make sure my back up is ready for a long run. Usually, I'd get home and give my baby a tune up so I could take her out again, but with a shorter deadline, I'll have to take my Harley Super glide instead of old faithful. The seat's not as comfortable, but it'll do.

Entering my mud room through the shop door, I remove my cut and gently hang it on one of the hooks lining the panel wall before plopping down on the foot bench to remove my boots. Sitting back up, I hear a scrape sound from somewhere. Pulling my pistol from my back slowly and switching the safety off, I bring it up to my chest, tucked tight, at the ready. Steps softened by thick socks are a blessing, but if I need to really move, I'll have no traction on the finished concrete floors. The faint glow from above the stove is the only light illuminating my space. I make it three steps before I notice the bottle of Macallan 18 and one of my highball glasses sitting on the marble countertop, a stool's been moved, and the glass is empty. I don't lower my pistol as I wait in the daunting silence to see who let themselves into my home.

From the darkness of my living room, I hear the clink of ice and whirl around, gun aimed.

"There's no need for the dramatics Dean." Rolling my eyes, I lower my pistol, tucking it back into the waistband of my jeans.

"Jesus Christ Jora, I could have shot you."

"But you didn't. Pour yourself a drink and join me." He levels his stony gaze at me, lifting one leg so his ankle rests across his other knee. He's completely unflappable. I hate poker nights with this fucker.

"Why are you sitting in the dark like a creature of the night? Also, dickbag, this is my house, I don't need an invitation, though I'm not sure how you crossed the threshold without one." Laughing at my own joke, I move to the island, grab the glass and pour two fingers worth of the fine scotch and throw it back, embracing the smoothness of the liquor and then the burn.

"Figured it was time we had a chat you grumbly bastard."

I scoff as I open the ice maker, grab a few cubes and add them to my glass before pouring another finger's worth of scotch. "A chat?"

"That's what I said. I'm not in the habit of repeating myself. You know this."

I make my way to my living room and flip on a lamp. Just because he wants to sit in the dark like a bat, doesn't mean I do. Settling into one of my armchairs across from him, I mirror his position. Lifting the glass to my forehead, I rub it across my temple; hoping the ice will soothe the blooming headache. I arch a brow at Jora, an indicator I'd like him to continue.

He takes a sip before setting the glass on one of my end tables.

No coaster. Typical.

"I hear you're going to NOLA." It's not a question.

"I'm taking Donnie with me."

"I know."

"And?" When he openly smirks at me, I snap, "Jora. I'm tired. Tell me why you're here."

"Very well." His expression darkens, "I've heard an interesting tidbit, thought you'd like to hear it."

"Do tell."

This piques my interest. As the club lawyer, Jora gets the first bits on anything and everything. People talk, and if you grease enough pockets, they'll sing. Jora being Jora, well he'll take his fists to someone for information quicker than offering money. If he wants to know something, he learns it. Dark mother fucker this one. But he's my best friend. So, he gets a pass.

"I heard there's a particular bar down there our friends are spending a lot of time in. Might be worth checking out." I asked him not to be vague, he's pushing it.

"Jora. Spell it out for me, we're not all on your level." Playing to his ego usually works wonders.

He smiles sharply, "While that is true, I've never felt you to be intellectually beneath me Dean. You know this."

"I know, but as I've said I'm fucking tired J, and I've got to head out bright and ugly. Cut me a break and just tell me what you know."

"Fine, fine. You're no fun. When's the last time you got laid?" He cuts in again before I can snarl at him. "Never mind, I know. You'd prefer your hand to anyone else." Raising his hands in a surrender.

"Fuck you, Jora." I snipe back at him. He laughs darkly.

"Alright, I'll stop. What I'm trying to say is you need to check this place out. I've asked Petey what's so special about it, he says nothing aside from good booze and a 'sexy Latina owner', his words not mine. Point being, when you get down there, you need to visit. Not sure if they're a front, or if the Russian's are taking turns banging the chick, but either way, something about it smells off."

"Have you told Prez?" I ask.

"I was on the phone with him before I came here, right after you went apeshit and threatened a sweet butt. Told him I was making a surprise visit, so he gave me the honors of relaying the message. If anything, you'll get some good drinks out of it and oh!" he looks at me excitedly, "I hear they've got live bands too, so you'll even get a show. Wouldn't that be nice? I know how much you love music."

"Fuck all the way off J." I snarl at him, before reigning myself in and asking resigned, "What's the name of this place?"

He doesn't react to my outburst, the patience of a saint this one. He picks invisible lint from his pressed slacks before answering me. "The Black Cat."

"The Black Cat?" I ask, just to be a dick. He rolls his eyes.

"What have I said that bears repeating? It's like you're not even listening to me Dean." He whines, faking a pout before getting serious. Leaning forward, arms on his thighs, fingers laced. He speaks slowly, enunciating like I'm a common dunce. I'd take offense, but at this point in my day, I don't give a shit. "Go to the bar. Take Donnie. Don't wear your cuts. Get a feel for the place. Use Donnie's ridiculous charm on the bar owner, figure out why the Russians would be frequenting the joint and report back. It's not that hard Dean. Colin shouldn't have to make the trip down if we do this right. If he shows up there, and it's a full house - of the Russian variety- there will be bloodshed. We need to avoid that if we can. Do your thing and let me know."

I eye him critically, he's stressed. If you know where to look, you can tell. His shirt is unbuttoned, he's sans tie. There's the slightest strain showing in the corner of his eyes, the way he ticks his jaw. He knows I'm making an assessment -and knowing Jora, he's unhappy with what I'm reading.

"What's bothering you really?" My voice lowers, taking on a serious edge.

"I'm not sure yet, but there's something we're missing. I love puzzles Dean. But I absolutely hate it when I don't have all the pieces. If Mihailo was going to start a war, he'd have done it already. He's waiting for something. Something big. I just don't know what yet. None of this makes sense."

I nod in contemplation. "That's what Pop's surmised. You think he's waiting for Colin to show before he strikes?"

He releases a heavy sigh, "I don't know what I think. McGregor stays holed up in his Chicago fortress, everyone knows that. He doesn't have to show himself when he has loyal, capable men to do his bidding. I've even asked Thorne if there's been any three-letter agency chatter. He said no. What good is it having a federal agent for a friend if he's no use to us?" He slumps back dramatically in his chair, picks up his glass and sips slowly.

We descend into comfortable silence, and I rub my hand along the leather armrest, going over what I know about the situation. I was just a kid when the Russian's last rose up, but Mihailo, he was older. He'd have been 15 at the time. The eldest of Vasiliy's sons would remember clearly what it felt like, watching my father and Colin kill his father. The details I know are murky. What I've always been told is that Mihailo's father instigated a coup d'état within the Irish brotherhood in retaliation for some transgression committed by Colin. Up until that point, the two men had been close friends. I've never learned exactly what the transgression was, although there's a rumor it started with Colin McGregor's wife. Mihailo has been taking care of his mother and brothers since then, on top of slowly rebuilding the Medvedev Bratva. The man he is now, in a word, calculating. We've lost shipments to him throughout the years, we've lost men. Both Irish and MC brothers alike. He doesn't discriminate. Always staying steps ahead of us, until eight years ago, tensions were at an all-time high when everything just... stopped. He stuck to his territory, we stuck to ours. There was an unspoken agreement to keep to ourselves. But in the last six months, something's changed. Hopefully in New Orleans I'll find some answers.

Snapping out of my thoughts, I address Jora. "I'm going to shower and sleep. I'll link up with Donnie in the morning. We'll visit the bar, and I'll keep you posted. Happy?"

"Supremely." He replies dryly.

I don't wait for him to leave, as I head to my room, I call over my shoulder. "See yourself out. Leave the bottle." His only response is more laughter.

I need sleep. I've got shit to do tomorrow.

CHAPTER THREE
Dean

We've been in New Orleans for an hour and I'm already sick of it. We pull up to the Saints MC gate and wait for entry; a prospect meets us, and while I can hear the music from here, he makes sure to let us know there's a celebration of life going on for Pete Sr and we're welcome to join. From there, he shows us to the guest cottage we'll stay in for the duration of our trip. It's not too shabby, better than staying at a motel. Two bedrooms, a Jack and Jill bathroom between and a small kitchenette with a coffee maker built into the wall. Points for the Saints, they even stocked the fridge. All the necessities two growing boys need. After Don and I took turns showering and changing, we figured we'd check out the celebration.

Two words: shit show.

Walking in, Don and I look at each other in disbelief. It's been a minute since I've visited this charter, clearly, they do things differently than we do. There were more sweet butts here than

I'd ever seen in one room. Weed smoke hung heavy in the air. Two MC brothers were fighting in front of some dart boards and there was a threesome happening on one of the leather sofas across from the pool tables. It's total fucking pandemonium.

I give it a moment to see if anyone questions our presence, surely someone is going to notice two strangers in their club? Right? We'd been standing there for five minutes before I test the waters with a roar, "Where the fuck is Petey?" Startling everyone, several guns are drawn.

Oh, now we're getting somewhere.

Donnie and I don't reach for our own weapons, I'm doubtful these guys could hit a target with the state they're in anyway. This is just pitiful.

"Who the fuck are you?" One supremely inebriated brother asks me. I eyeball his cut as he sways on his feet, seems his name is Jorge. Ignoring him for now, I shake my head, upper lip curled in disgust and turn to Donnie. *'Can you believe this shit'* I'm asking with my eyes. He shrugs his shoulders in a *'what are you gonna do'* gesture, scratching the back of his head.

Tongue in cheek, I stare up at the ceiling momentarily, looking for all the answers there before addressing the dumb fucker who's getting entirely too close to me.

"I'm Dean Graham. Ravens VP, out of Ravenswood." Clenching my teeth, I ask again forcefully, "Where is Petey?"

Jorge slurs back, "He's dead."

With an exaggerated eyeroll I bite back, "No shit. Junior. Not Senior."

Dumb fuck Jorge takes in our cuts with squinted eyes before they widen like a light bulb going off in that brain of his. Seems he's finally figured out who we are and the reason for this visit.

Clearing his throat, he mutters "Oh uh sorry, right this way."

Gesturing for us to follow with a hooked thumb over his

shoulder before turning on his heel and trudging toward the staircase. Don and I follow dutifully, when we reach the top, he tells us to go right and it's the last door on the left. We hear moans the closer we get. Before Donnie has a chance to knock, I'm brushing past him, shouldering my way into the office. Petey's sitting at his desk, head thrown back in ecstasy, mouth open and hands fisted in a blonde woman's hair as he fucks her mouth. He's so into what they're doing, he hasn't even noticed our arrival.

Fucking typical.

I'm stewing and this trip has barely started. Donnie looks at me pleadingly. "Don't. This isn't our place. They want to get fucked up and run themselves into the ground. It's on them."

At the end of his sentence, Petey climaxes with a groan, and that kids, is the straw that finally breaks this camel's back. I pull my pistol from it's holster and pop two rounds into the ceiling in quick succession. Never breaking my brother's eye. Petey screams, the sweet butt screams and Donnie rolls his eyes at my feral grin. Then the thunder of footsteps reaches our ears. Moving quickly, before the whole club can clamber our way, I gracefully maneuver around Petey's desk, grab the blonde –who gives me a saucy smile- and gently push her from the room. I lock the door before turning around and leveling Petey Brandt with a gaze full of menace. He gulps, hands raised in surrender and dick still half-mast.

"What are you doing Dean?" he asks, voice shaking, brown eyes wide, pupils blown with fear.

"What am I doing? Testing your security.... What the fuck are you doing Pete? We've talked about this. You can't let these guys run wild without security."

At my chastising, Donnie whips his head in my direction. "You've talked about this? When?"

Not bothering to acknowledge him, I level Pete with a dark look.

"Pete. We walked right in, and nobody stopped us."

My brother snaps his fingers at me, and I finally turn in annoyance.

"Hello, when did you talk about security with another MC?"

Shrugging indifferently, I give him a vague answer. "I ran into Petey some months back. Gave him some advice, it's no big deal."

Bringing my attention back to Petey, I arch a brow. I'm still waiting for an answer. He stutters out, "We're still in mourning man. This is the last hurrah ya know, before shit gets serious."

A fist strikes his door harshly, snagging my attention. One of his men yells through the wood, "Prez you alright?"

I cut my eyes back in Pete's direction. "Well, are you?"

He yells out, "We're good. That was me, accident. Carry on."

There are a few grumbled protests before we hear them leave.

I level him with a hard look, "You going to have your shit together come tomorrow?"

"Yeah man, like I said, this is the last party for a while."

"Good, because we've got shit to do. You asked for my help, so I'm here." I angle my head in Donnie's direction. "That's my brother Donnie. He's with me. This isn't how we operate, if it's a problem, we'll go home. Understood?"

"No, not at all. No problem. It's not usually like this man. I'm sorry I didn't meet you at the gate. I wasn't sure what time to expect you and honestly didn't think it'd be this soon." He's tugging his jeans back onto his hips and fumbling with his zipper.

I stop him with a hand. "No need to get up. Just know we're going to be talking tomorrow. There's a lot to go over. This is bigger than you realize Pete. For now, we're going to head out for a bit." hesitating, I debate the next question, fucking Jora, "Now tell me, where can I find The Black Cat?"

CHAPTER FOUR

Sage

Jericho's been out of the house for a full day and I'm going stir crazy missing her. Keeping myself busy, I started my project list with a trip to the grocery store, making sure to stock up on wine, because let's be real. I'll need it. Then I spent most of my afternoon finally mowing and putting the rest of her bedroom together. She's upgraded beds since we moved from our small apartment. Getting rid of the twin she had and replacing it with a full. It truly makes me want to cry, but she loved this one when we went furniture shopping, it's a day bed, complete with a canopy. Beautiful lavender gossamer lays on either side of the frame and the thousand and one throw pillows look amazing with the comforter's color scheme. My girl is growing up. I put so much work into her room, needing everything to be just so. Her future is beautiful if I can just keep it that way.

We're safe here. Safer than we've been anywhere else. As I sit on her bed, one of her plushies tucked to my chest, I think about the future. While I'd love nothing more than to share it with Dean, I wonder if there's some truth to Tessa's advice? Do I need to move on? The thought of another man touching me after all this time fills me with dread. I've never wanted anyone else, and I miss him fiercely. But I can't. He'd be in too much danger. I can't pull him into my mess. I sigh out to the quiet room. Before my thoughts get a chance to turn too heavy, my cell dings from the living room.

Setting her plushie back gently I drag ass to check my messages. There's a barrage of them now, ding after ding. Already knowing who it is, I roll my eyes.

Tessa: What do?

Tessa: I know what you're not doing.

Tessa: You're not here.

Tessa: You're at home wallowing. Come here and wallow with me instead.

Tessa: I mean it. If you don't show up in the next 25 minutes, I will show up and show out!

Tessa: Don't sit at home and drink by yourself bitch. Come to the bar and drink with me.

I read her text vomit before sending off one of my own.

Harlow: Don't tell me what to do.

Tessa: ......

Harlow: What?

Tessa: I'm the boss, remember? It's literally what I do. Now bring that sweet ass to TBC and drink with me.

Fuck it.

I could use a night out of my own head.

Harlow: Fine. You talked me into it.

Tessa: Attagirl.

Hurrying to get ready, I slipped into a pair of high waisted skinny jeans, ripped at the knees and threw on an olive-green bandeau top before spritzing some *cool blue perfume* and fluffing my coppery curls. Running some oil through the ends, I consider cutting it but quickly change my mind. Right now, it's the longest it's ever been, the ends just brushing my waist. Can't say I don't love it. Because I do, even if some days it's a right pain in my ass. Deciding to leave it down, I moved on to my face. I rarely wear makeup, so I just dab on a little BB cream and blend in a barely there liquid blush, embracing my freckles. Before leaving I apply a bit of mascara and throw on some lip balm. Good as I'll ever be. Slipping into my lifted Vans, I grab my crossbody and head out.

30 minutes later, I'm shouldering my way through The Black Cat. It's a Monday, the place isn't overly crowded, but it's still summer, so the college crowd is insane no matter the day of the week. I see Tess sitting on a bar stool, faced pressed to her phone, fingers flying furiously over the keyboard. When I'm close, I see that she's texting me. Telling me to 'hurry the fuck up'. At my tap on her shoulder, she whips around on her bar stool and takes me in with wide eyes, smiling appreciatively.

"Maldita mamá, te ves bien!" She jumps from her seat and pulls me in for a hug, taking a big whiff of my perfume and groaning out loud. "Tú también hueles bien!"

Laughing while easing myself from her grip, I ask. "Did you get me a drink?"

"I did, but then you were taking so long, so I drank it."

She gives me a lopsided grin. It's rare to see this side of her. Usually, Tess and I are all work, no play.... But tonight, she's excited and I'm excited too just being in her presence. You know when you meet someone on a soul deep level? You just click?

That's the bond I have with her.

Sisters by choice, not blood.

Pulling out a stool beside her, I sit and raise my hand to get Antony's attention. He's one of my favorites. When he finally makes it to us, he takes me in with wide eyes and fangirls for just a moment. I adore him, my favorite hype person.

"Oh, my goshhhhh! Harlow, you look scrumptious! You have to sing tonight! Show off this cuteness girl." His energy is contagious, I can't help but smile along with him.

"I might." I say with a sly grin.

"She will, if I have anything to say about it." Tess shoots Antony a wink before ordering us both a round of Long Islands.

"How much have you had to drink Tessie?" I side eye her.

"Why? Are you offering to take me home?" she asks, waggling her eyebrows at me.

"I've not met my charitable donations for the year, so I suppose if I must." I sigh dramatically, she nudges my shoulder with hers in a playful reprimand.

"I've had a few mami, but I'm good. Come on, let's go find an empty table." The foot traffic is really starting to pick up, bartenders running from one end to the other. Tessa is a stickler about her one night off a week. She won't jump in and help them, adamant that everyone needs time. That's why we have the crew we do. Implicit trust in their capabilities is key. We make our way across the room, a quiet alcove close to the courtyard. Less light makes its way here, giving a sense of privacy. Tess and I order a few more rounds from a passing server, I'm starting to feel them, and my inhibitions slip. We've played four rounds of quarters and laughed and talked, then laughed some more. It's the best night I've had in a while. I'm definitely buzzed, positive we'll be ubering to my house and picking my truck up in the morning.

Tessa's gone to the bathroom a few minutes when a lumbering

giant of a man takes a seat across from me. He's massive, a white button up straining across his broad chest. If I had to guess, I'd say an inch or two over six foot with a head full of tousled chestnut hair, thick brows set above sapphire eyes that seem to sparkle with mischief, and the sharpest jaw covered in five o' clock shadow. When I realize I've been caught staring, I can't fight the blush coming over me, and he smiles. It's beautiful, plush lips pull back to reveal perfect teeth, but there's something sharp about it too, predatory, it reminds me of *Bruce*, from *Finding Nemo*.

"I saw you sitting in the dark by yourself, I'd like to buy you a drink."

It's not a question.

Where are my words? *You don't want a drink. Tell him you don't want one.*

"Sure." *What the fuck is wrong with you? You didn't want a drink from him.*

His shark's smile gets wider, he signals a server, when Nikki pops by, ready to take our order, he asks what I'm having. I can't answer. I'm lost. Too fucking blitzed to figure out what day it even is.

When I finally recall what's in the glass in front of me, I snap my fingers like a dumb ass. *Very Sherlock Holmes.*

Elementary, my dear Watson. Pfft. You're an idiot Sage.

"A Long Island." I answer proudly.

Nikki looks at me like I've lost my mind, I just shake my head and cover my eyes with my hands. I don't even hear what he's ordered himself. My awkwardness is too loud. Feeling a gentle tug on my fingers, I dare a peek through half lowered lids. He looks concerned.

It's valid.

I do look crazy.

I'm not going to tell him it's because he's the first man who's struck me stupid in eight years. *Holy. Fucking. Shit. It's been eight years since I've been with a man.*

"Are you alright?" He asks me softly.

I would say I'm out of it, but truthfully, I don't think I've been 'in it' for a long time.

Shit don't say that Sage. You've got more brains than this.

"I'm okay, sorry about that. I think the drink went to my head. I've had little to eat today."

Where the fuck is Tess? I need a buffer.

"Don't apologize. Would you like some jambalaya? This place makes the best I've had."

This I can work with. Talk about the bar Sage.

"Oh, you come here often?" I ask, in what I hope is a flirtatious way, but most likely... not.

"I do actually, well, I guess that's not entirely true, I've recently started." I catch the faintest trace of an accent when he speaks. European maybe? With the number of drinks I've had, I can't place it for sure.

"Where are you from?" I ask curiously.

"I'm from Vegas, travelling for work, haven't been in New Orleans long, just a few weeks. The clubs back home, they don't feel like this. Here, there's possibility in the air, like anything could happen." Those sapphire eyes glint again.

Suddenly feeling bashful, I tuck a stray hair behind my ear, "The owner is my best friend. I help her run this place."

"You and your friend have done a fantastic job. It's truly something." Just then, Nikki interrupts us with the drink order. She gives him something that looks to be vodka on the rocks and hands me my Long Island. I smiled at her in thanks. When his back is turned, she widens her eyes, giving me two thumbs up and a wink before carrying on. I see her intercept Tessa as she's making her way to the bar. Hooking her arm through my friends, she leans in and whispers something in her ear. When Tessa's shocked gaze whips in my direction, her jaw drops and then morphs into a lascivious grin.

The Adonis across from me holds his drink out in cheers, drawing my attention back to him, "What are we drinking to?" I ask.

"New friends, I hope." He smiles shyly.

This man has never been shy a day in his life. But that's none of my business.

"I don't even know your name."

"It's Michael. What's yours?"

"Harlow." I raise my glass and clink it to his. We both drink. I catch his gaze wander to my lips as I slip my straw into my mouth. His eyes darken and my core heats.

"Now," He takes my small hand in one of his massive ones, "you know my name and I know yours." He purrs, "Friends?"

I giggle. I. Fucking. Giggle.

Like some vapid schoolgirl.

I can feel every bit of my face turning crimson. *My inner goddess recoils from the embarrassment.* He knows the effect he's having on me, biting down on that lush bottom lip, his voice drops low, sexy. "You're not what I was expecting."

Before I have time to question what that means, I hear Tessa's intoxicated voice over the microphone.

"Boys and girls! In the house tonight we have our very own Songbird living her best life at The Black Cat! Let's see if we can talk our girl Harlow into coming up and gracing us with her talented tongue! For all of you who've never been here before and refresher for those who have, I'd like to remind you about the *strict no recording policy* when my girl here takes the stage.

Don't make me play bad cop, I'd much prefer to be cuffed than do the cuffing." She winks saucily, playing up the crowd.

Oh no.

It's mortifying when she does this, when I look back to gauge Michael's reaction, he's gone. Like he was never here. Then the chanting starts, and I'm trying to figure out how I can get out of it.

CHAPTER FIVE
Dean

Donnie and I borrow one of the cages from the Saints. Promising the prospect, we'd bring her back in one piece as he tosses us the keys. It's an old school Chevy Blazer, square body. I love classics if I'm honest. All black and chrome, smooth as butter leather interior. If I've got to leave my bike tonight, at least I'm in something this nice. Unable to find parking close by, I pulled into the nearest parking garage, and we trek the two blocks to get in line.

As we approach, I see immediately this place is on another level. I can hear the instrumentals, the sounds of indie rock spilling onto the sidewalk. Donnie and I don't wait in line too long before we're bustling our way through the crowd. I'd rather not fight my way to the bar, noticing there are plenty of servers milling around, I wait until one catches my eye, I lift my hand, indicating we're grabbing a table, and she nods. Luckily, we found an empty one closer to the front door, farthest from the stage. It gives me a good vantage for the most part. I can see who's coming in and most of the room. I can't tell for sure, but it looks like there's a courtyard space, if the rolling doors are any sign, there's outdoor seating as well.

This doesn't look like your typical Bratva hang out. Nothing screams 'back-room deals' to me thus far. Even so, the prettiest flowers can be poisonous too. We've only been in here 10 minutes; the night is still young. The band is good, really good. Servers mill about, doing their job quickly and efficiently. Donnie and I had drinks less than five minutes after our orders were taken. This place feels loved and the employees seem to enjoy being here and what they do. It speaks to good management and ownership. The air here isn't cloying or overpowering. There's no sickly scent of cigarettes or weed. I can smell the undertone of something, it's pleasant, familiar, but I'm unable to put my finger on it.

I'm distracted by the ambience when Donnie nudges me with his elbow softly, never moving his head. Following his line of sight, we see two burly men at the bar. Not your average college boy either. They're scanning the room but trying their best to blend in.

Donnie cocks his head to the side and under his breath asks, "Bodyguards or rugby players?"

"Not the rugby type. Keep an eye out."

I watch the flow of everything. The bartenders work smoothly, you can tell there's a system in place. Mixing and tossing bottles in the air. It's something alright. I'm bringing my whiskey to my lips when I hear Donnie's sudden intake of breath.

"Who is that?"

"Who is who?"

"That."

He grabs my chin and turns my head in the direction he's staring, squishing my cheeks. Pulling my face from his fist, I finally focus on who he's talking about.

"She's the owner. Jora sent me her picture when we were on our way."

"What's her name?" He's fucking spellbound.

"Funny you should ask, Jora said you should work your charms on her, figure out why the Bratva is here so often."

He cranks his head so fast; I'm surprised it didn't break. "Seriously?"

"Yeah man, go buck wild. Her names Tessalynn Sanchez."

He scans her slowly from head to toe and hear him mutter a quiet 'fuck me' under his breath before turning around in his seat, more serious than I've ever seen him.

"I'm not going to go buck wild with her, I'm going to fucking marry that woman."

He polishes off the rest of his drink and straightens his shirt before leaving me stunned stupid at the table. For a moment, it takes me back, the way he just reacted. Insta love, insta obsession. That's how it felt when I looked at my Songbird. I'd have done anything for her. If she'd asked me to carve out my own heart I would have. Her name was already written on it. Sitting back, I watch Donnie approach the owner and strike up a conversation. She smiles politely and then throws her head back laughing loudly at what he's just said, still smiling, she pats him on the shoulder like a small child, then she winks and glides away. He watches her retreating for a moment before shaking his head and returning to the table invigorated despite what was a definite rejection.

I can't hide my amusement when he takes his seat beside me.

"How'd that go, Romeo?" I ask just as I take another sip of the whiskey, damn it's good.

He's still staring off into the distance, probably looking for her. "I told her I was going to marry her."

Somehow, I managed not to spit out my drink, though barely. "Are you serious?"

"Deadly." he affirms.

The thing is, I believe him. Before I can chime in and rib him some more, the object of his desires hops onto the stage, the indie band is taking a break and she's getting ready to make some sort of announcement. Don straightens in his seat, sitting at attention, completely captivated by her. She is a beautiful woman. Full hips, narrow waist. Decent breasts, I can admit to that. Long dark hair and it's pin straight. Golden skin and soulful caramel eyes.

My brother's a goner. For fucking sure.

When she's sure she's gotten the crowd calmed down a bit, she grabs the microphone and walks over to the side closest to the rolling door, hips swinging as she goes. This woman knows how to use her body, she's enchanting. We watch as she smirks mischievously at someone down below before addressing the rest of the patrons.

"Boys and girls! In the house tonight we have our very own Songbird living her best life at The Black Cat! Let's see if we can talk our girl Harlow into coming up and gracing us with her talented tongue! For all of you who've never been here before and refresher for those who have, I'd like to remind you about the *strict no recording policy* when my girl here takes the stage. Don't make me play bad cop, I'd much prefer to be cuffed than do the cuffing."

The chanting and calls for this person to sing start at once. Feet stomp over the dance floor in thunderous waves. Across the room, I barely make out the server who brought us our drinks, she's dragging what appears to be a reluctant woman towards the stage. A woman who shakes her head vehemently. I'm unable to make out her face or features, that area of the bar is too dark, but I can see her head tilt to the ceiling and imagine a slew of protests leave her lips. Curiosity peaked; I'm straining in my seat, trying to catch a glimpse of her. From afar, she looks delicate.

Watch. Listen.

Alarm bells are going off in my head.

My heart starts to race, I grab Donnie's wrist, not taking my eyes off the reluctant woman. I ask my brother, "Did she say Songbird?"

"I think so, yeah. What are the odds?"

All the air leaves my lungs in a great exhale. Donnie eyes me, concerned.

It can't fucking be. It can't.

When the stage lights change and the first rays of a red glow hit her, *I see her.*

How is this possible?

Fuck me sideways.

She's alive. She's here. Beautiful and alive. She. Is. Alive. She's alive. She's here.

Like a hammer in my chest, my heart beats uncomfortably. My brother slaps my shoulder, hard, but I don't move.

I can't. I'm stuck. Unable to comprehend what my eyes are telling me.

This isn't possible.

It shouldn't be possible, yet I'm seeing her.

Right now, she's fucking gravity, and I'm caught in it, in her.

Her copper hair is in its natural state, curls on top of curls tumbling down her back and over her shoulders. It's longer than I've ever seen it. Blonde highlights break apart the warm color. She's grown into her beauty, that's for sure. The woman across the bar is simply stunning.

I trail my eyes from her feet up, clad in classic Vans that give her stature just a bit of added lift. Her jeans hug her lean legs, and I can just make out the definition in her quads. Tessalynn pulls her into a hug, blocking my perusal.

She's alive. She's alive. She's. Fucking. Alive.

And somebody lied to me.

"Dean, Dean, fuck man, are you seeing this?"

Yeah, I'm seeing it alright. But I can't speak. My tongue is a lead weight in my mouth. My throat strangled with disbelief.

I'm held hostage in this moment.

I can't do anything but take her in.

I'm afraid to blink.

If I do, will she disappear? No. This is real.

Tessalynn steps away and I can really look my fill. Sage has grown ten times more beautiful through the years, but there's no mistaking, it's her. I don't understand how this is possible.

Someone hands her a guitar. The microphone is adjusted to reach her while she sits on a little stool, one foot kicked up on it, the other on the floor. The crowd, knowing what's coming, quiets down.

Her cheeks are flushed as she addresses the patrons. "For those of you unfamiliar, my name's Harlow. I'm not going to do a cover tonight." They start to complain, but I can tell it's all in good spirits.

They're familiar with her.

With a graceful smile on her face, she continues as if she can't hear them.

"No, no y'all. I'm going to sing one of mine. I've got someone who lays heavy in my heart. So, I'm going to tell you all about him."

There are a few cat calls and 'awws' when she says that last bit, but as she starts to pluck the acoustic guitar, they shut up and listen. The slow notes of the guitar encourage several patrons to move onto the dance floor below her. Couples pair off and sway to the rhythm.

It's taking every bit of my restraint not to go to her, to demand answers. The beast in my chest is clawing his way up my throat. With a centering breath, I push him down. I can't fuck this up.

Donnie has an iron clad grip on my shoulder. I'm letting him ground me. We both know it. When she opens her mouth, the raspy melody takes me back, and I let it pull me under.

We've been at Thorne's house for several hours now, after getting back from taking the gator out. I'm waiting on the porch for Jora to get here and for Thorne to grab his trunks. We're spending the rest of the day at the pond. It's a hot sonofabitch and I can't wait to jump off the dock. Only two weeks left until school starts and I plan to make the most of it. I'm picking the petals off one of Hattie's roses when I hear it - the softest noise flows through the air. At first, I think someone's whispering, maybe one of the guys fucking with me? I concentrate, ears perked, trying to listen better. It's slow and sad, but gritty, raw somehow. I meander to my feet and slowly make my way towards the weeping willow. Following the sound, I stay off the gravel and walk on the grass to soften my steps. I don't want to scare off whoever this is. The closer I get, the clearer it is. Someone's singing 'Hallelujah'. But it doesn't sound like you'd hear it in a church, it's heartbreaking. I move the curtain of weeping wisps and step into the shroud of shadows. It's like another world here. With slices of sunlight streaking through the branches, roots as big as my leg carved the ground into pieces. The tree's grown low enough for climbing. This is a cool spot, how have I not noticed before? I'm wondering about the best way to climb up when I see her. She's like an angel, sitting midway up the branches. The sun hits her, illuminating copper hair. It's shorter now than it was last summer. Only to her nape. Curls wild and free. Her back is to me, she keeps singing. I haven't given myself away, I don't want to disturb her. It's a revelation. I've seen Sage around a few times, even dug her out of the cornfield when Hattie couldn't find her. She's around 11 now, I think. I make my way slowly to get a better look at her, I need to see if this is really her singing or if she's playing music somehow. When I duck under one of the lower branches, I freeze. Her lips are moving, her eyes are closed, dark lashes touching the tops of her cheeks. Her voice is powerful, it's shocking, she's always so quiet. Thorne says I need to stay away from her, 'nothing good can come of it'. He's warned us all away. I can't lie, my thoughts have drifted to her often the last couple of years, but I've held my tongue. She always looks so sad. I don't need Thorne to wonder why I'm asking about his little sister; it would mess with our friendship. Plus, she's a kid. But right now, as I stare at this little songbird, perched in the tree, I don't care who she is. I need to hear her sing again and again. When she opens her eyes, they're the brightest I've ever seen them. A blue so pretty, it's like looking into the endless sea. I can't breathe. For the first time in my 13 years, I understand what beauty is.

I'm jolted back to the present, catching the tail end of her song. I didn't catch all the lyrics, but the end. It resonates with me.

'There is no heart for me like yours,

There is no love for you like mine.

You made the fall feel like flying'

Silent tears track down her face and I want nothing more than to wipe them away and hold her. The crowd goes wild. Clapping and whistling. Breaking from the spell is harder than I like, but I have to. Throwing some money on the table, I grab Donnie's arm, pulling him with me while there's a distraction. I can't let her see me yet. I need to find out everything about her. Who she is now, what her life is like.

Why is she here?

There was a reason she let me think she's been dead these long years. Now that the shock has worn off, I can admit I'm angry. The betrayal stings.

But that song, that fucking song. Was it about me? Or someone else?

I need answers.

When we make it to the truck, I pull out my cell to call Jora.

"She's alive." Not bothering to greet him, my breath is choppy.

He's quiet, at first, I assume it's due to the shock. There's only one 'she' I could be talking about. Then I hear the storm brewing in his voice. "I know."

"What do you mean?" I just found out. How could he possibly know?

"I've got Thorne here."

"And? What does he have to do with it? I'm telling you, she's here. She's alive and she's here." I'm rambling. I can't stop.

"Dean. I know. I really do. Calm down." He blows out a ragged breath, "Thorne just dropped it on me an hour ago. I've been trying to figure out the best way to tell you, naturally, you beat me to it. Universe and mystery am I right?" he laughs dryly, "Your girl's in trouble D. She's been in trouble all along, and now they're in her backyard."

"Explain." I'm clenching the phone so tight, it's a wonder it hasn't snapped.

I hear a scuffle, and Thorne cuts in before Jora can say anything else.

"D... I know this is a mind fuck. But broth-."

I cut him off darkly. "You lied to me."

I'm falling apart at the seams.

"She's my baby sister. My loyalty will always be to her. I had to. You may not understand now, but you will. At the end of the day, we're brothers. We. Are. Brothers. Whether you see it or not, I did what I had to. While you're there, promise me you'll look after her, that you'll keep her safe." He sounds desperate.

The betrayal is a dull knife digging into my back. Thorne's been one of my best friends since before our balls dropped. Part of me wants to believe he lied for a good reason. But the other part, that's pure rage.

I growl into the phone. "Now that I know she's here, I'm not leaving without her. As for you and me, after this, we're done."

With a defeated sigh, he says, "Me and Jora are heading your way in the next couple of days. We'll let you know when we make it."

Without a response, I drop the call and lean back against the headrest. Donnie, who's been listening to everything this whole time, finally speaks.

"D. I've got you. You know?"

"Yeah man, I know." I blow out a breath, rocking my head gently a few times into the headrest before sitting up and starting the truck.

"Donnie, I'm going to drop you at the clubhouse and come back. I need to find out where she's staying."

We both knew I could just ask Jora; he'd get the info from Thorne. But I don't want to. This is something I want to do on my own. There's a desperate need to be close to her, and I'm not willing to pull myself from her orbit.

"Whatever you need Dean. Just don't do anything drastic." I blow a raspberry and laugh, but there's no humor in it.

"Drastic enough to fake my own death and leave my loved ones to mourn for eight years? That drastic?"

"Point taken." he winces, "I just meant, don't end up in jail."

"That I can't promise you, but if I do…. call Thorne."

He owes me.

My brother chuckles, before we make our way back to Saints MC I need to grab some coffee. I've got a long night of stalking to do.

CHAPTER SIX
Sage, Age 14

We've got two weeks left until Christmas, which means I've lived with the Masons for ten years now, it's official. Ten years since I'd been dropped on my Aunt Hattie's doorstep in the dead of night. 'For my safety'. What a crock of shit. Can't say I've ever really felt safe. But according to my aunt, mama was married to a bad man, a man who'd be looking for me, a man who hurt her and would do terrible, awful things to me if I was ever found. I sometimes wonder if that life would be preferable. I've been a verbal – and sometimes literal- punching bag since I was old enough to question things. Between the alcohol and the misery my Aunt Hat permeates, I no longer accept her words at face value.

What was my life?

What was my mother's name, my father's?

These are answers I don't have, but desperately need. There's a block from before, I was too young when they left me. My dreams are usually filled with smoke and blood, in them, I'm always running, and I don't know why. Most nights I wake in a panic, a muscle memory only my body knows tied to some trauma I've suppressed. The first time the dreams plagued me, I tried seeking comfort in my aunt, she quickly let me know I was looking in the wrong place. After that, Thorne and Fern, Hattie's children, took turns sharing their beds at night. When they started calling me their sister, Hattie didn't dispute it. When I asked why? She shrugged, letting me know it was easier to sell the story, then instructed me to shut my mouth and go with it.

Questions will get you killed.

Now that I'm older, I've done my research on mental defense mechanisms, understanding what it means, the night terrors are manageable, but sometimes my dreams leave a restlessness I can't shake. Case in point, tonight. It was new, I wasn't scared. On the contrary, I felt safe. There was a man, but I didn't know him. His smile reached his blue eyes as he held me high above him. My arms were spread wide, the dream was filled with joy. When I woke up sometime after 1am, tears were tracking down my face. No hysterics, no screams. I tried so hard to return to sleep, but no such luck. The dream left me with a deep ache, an intense longing curdling my chest. Waking up was heartbreaking. Deep down, I know they're not dreams, they're memories.

After tossing and turning for far too long, I slipped from my bed and threw on a pair of shoes while wrapping a throw blanket around my shoulders. Sneaking from the house is easy. Hattie drinks herself into a stupor most nights by 8pm and she's out for the count shortly after. It's only my siblings I've got to worry about following me. In my haste, my escape is sloppy. Instead of the trellis outside my bedroom, I tiptoe downstairs and use the kitchen door.

Over the years, I've come to learn that only walking the grounds or sitting under the willow tree's embrace can ease the madness inside me. Something about the way the world sleeps, it's peaceful. My brain isn't so loud at night. Starlight illuminated the path as I made my way. Slivers of frost covered every inch of the yard. It felt magical.

Humming quietly to myself to keep my chest warm, I listened as the frost crunched with every step I took. My breath caught in my throat when I heard the footsteps behind me. I wasn't alone. Whirling around, I expected to see Fern, she was a year younger than me, and I fully intended to send her on her way. If Hattie found out she'd snuck out, -because I snuck out- she'd be furious. I've heard time and again how I'm a bad influence. The only thing I'm guilty of is encouraging her to think for herself. With a reprimand on my tongue, I snap my mouth shut when I see it isn't Fern's blonde hair peeking through a black hoodie, it was someone much taller, someone who blends in with the night, someone who seemed to be born from it.

My brother's best friend, Dean Graham. I hadn't forgotten he was staying over for a few days during the holiday break. I'm usually painfully aware of him. He and Thorne, both sophomores in high school, are two years older than me. Thoughts of him vex me, he's the star in all my daydreams. Like a puzzle I can't solve, it's frustrating. I never know how to interpret Dean; from time to time, I catch him staring at me in that intense way of his. But he never gives me more than a gruff hello or pained glance when he notices I'm watching too. His eyes, set under dark brows, remind me of liquid silver. Simply stunning. They seem to glow like a predator in the night. I'm staring, I can't help it, like my soul is drawn to his.

As much as I enjoy seeing him, I'm angry with him too. He needs to get his shit together. Thorne mentioned a few weeks ago that I had a boyfriend.

Tommy Willis.

It didn't matter that Tommy wasn't really my boyfriend, he just wished he was. Point is, last week, Tommy got jumped, and his pitching arm was broken. No one could figure out who did it. But in my heart of hearts, I knew it was Dean. Anytime Thorne brought it up, I'd see the smallest smirk lift his lips.

Pausing my journey to the willow, I let him catch up to me. Not willing to risk calling out and waking anyone else. If Dean was here, it meant my brother wouldn't be far behind. When he made it three feet from me, he stopped. I looked over his shoulder, there was no movement from the house, and I realized he was alone. He looked nervous, chest heaving. His hands were in his hoodie pocket, jaw clenched tight as those silver eyes scanned me from head to toe.

When he started to open his mouth, I cut in before he had a chance to speak. "What are you doing out here?"

His head jerked back like I'd slapped him, and he looked at me baffled.

"I was going to ask you the same question. Have you been crying?" lifting one hand from his pocket and raising it to my face. He paused briefly before closing the distance, running the pad of his thumb over my cheek. The touch was warm, warmer than I'd been expecting. I sucked in a breath at the spark running through me on contact. I felt tongue tied. My heart was a hummingbird in my chest. He took another step closer, his eyes never leaving my face, while his thumb made soothing strokes across the apple of my cheek. So warm. In a daze, I was swaying.

Pulling his other hand from his hoodie, he slipped it under my blanket, palm encompassing my waist over my own sweater. He was steadying me. I still hadn't answered him. This was too much. Too emotional. With difficulty, I stepped back from him, missing the warmth at once. He looked at his hand curiously while rubbing his thumb and index finger together softly before tucking it back in his pocket. I wonder if he could feel it too? The charge.

Rocking back on his heels, he asks me again. "Are you okay Songbird?"

Songbird?

"Why would you call me that?" My question a whisper in the wind.

He rolls his lips, a furrow in his brow, "Because that's what you are, at least that's what you are to me."

"Since when?" I eye him skeptically and pull my bottom lip between my teeth.

He locks in on the movement before gesturing with his hand toward my tree. "Let's go under the willow, and I'll tell you."

I nod my head and continue to my original destination; while stealing glances of him walking at my side. When we make it to the swaying wisps, he reaches out and moves the iced curtain, letting me go under first. I find a nice spot, free of frost and sit, while he stands awkwardly, indecision warring on his face.

"You can sit by me. I won't bite." I chuckled quietly.

He mutters something sounding like 'I might' under his breath before dropping down beside me. The proximity feels like sitting on a livewire. He leaves about six inches between us. Well, that just won't do. It's different under the tree, the wind not as aggressive, still the cold touches us. I scooch closer to share his warmth. He stiffens, but as I settle beside him shoulder to shoulder, he slowly relaxes.

After a few tense moments, he breaks the silence. "You never answered me, are you alright?"

I nod my head, "I am. It's hard to sleep sometimes. When I can't sleep, I like to walk."

"You realize it's freezing outside?"

I laugh, but there's no humor in it. "The cold doesn't bother me much."

"Well, it bothers me, you could get sick." He growls back.

"Why do you care?" I ask, eyeing him curiously.

He shrugs, lazily. Realizing I'm not going to get an answer, I changed the subject.

"You called me Songbird; you owe me an explanation."

He tilts his head back against the tree trunk and watches the branches sway in the wintery breeze. Without looking at me, he says softly. "I watched you here one day. It was the end of summer; you were sitting on a branch. Like a bird. Singing." He drops his gaze to my face, mouth in a tight line.

"Ahh, so because I was singing, in a tree, Songbird is what you came up with?" I tuck my chin to my chest, looking up at him from under my lashes.

His face is full of emotion I can't decipher. He rasps out, "To answer your first question, I've always cared Sage. As for your nickname; you looked free. Beautiful. In that moment, you could have raised your arms wide and flown.... That's why I call you Songbird."

Like two magnets, we've drifted closer together as he speaks. Practically nose to nose. Both our chests heaving in sync. Bringing his hand back up slowly, he cups my face and tilts my chin. Angling me the way he wants me.

I feel like Icarus at this moment, there's fire in his silver eyes, he burns like the sun and I'm burning with him.

Suddenly, he lets me go, pulling back. Snapping me out of my revery and taking all the heat with him. Did I misread this? He shakes his head, curls his hands in a fist and I watch the moment pass. This is the most vulnerable I've ever seen Dean. Of course it wasn't meant to last.

If I go first, I'll save myself from embarrassment. As if he can ready my thoughts, Dean snaps out a hand, snagging my wrist before I can move away. Silver eyes stare back at me, they look almost pleading.

"You're Thorne's little sister. He's my best friend. He wouldn't want me to."

I snap back at him, "Is that why you beat up Tommy? Because I'm Thorne's little sister?"

He rolls his eyes and snarls, "Tommy was a shithead who was telling people he could get into your pants without trying. He deserved to have his arm broken, the little shits lucky that's all I did."

"You expect me to believe it wasn't simply because you were jealous?"

In a low murmur he replies, "You're Thorne's sister."

Oh, so that's what this is?

"You always do what Thorne wants?" I'm fuming. "The question is, what do you want? And don't fucking lie Dean. Don't be a coward. Own your shit."

Losing his patience, he barks, "Fine! You want the truth? For fucks sake, Sage, I've wanted to kiss you since the first time I heard you sing, right under this very willow tree, years ago."

I get in his face, intending to be challenging, instead my statement comes out breathless. "But you're scared."

He scoffs, "I'm not scared."

"No? I see the way you watch me Dean. If you're paying close enough attention, then you know I watch you too." I raise a brow, daring him to tell me different.

He lets go of my wrist and levels me with a dark look. "If I kiss you, that's it. You don't understand. I've obsessed over you for years Songbird." I wasn't expecting that. He goes on, "If I kiss you. You're mine."

Looking him in the eye, hoping he can see my sincerity. The answer is easy. "You dummy, I'm already yours. I've just been waiting for you to catch up."

He considers this for all of two seconds before he brings his mouth down to mine. The kiss is gentle and warm. Lips meeting in the softest of brushes. I'm sinking further as he bands an arm around my waist, the other going to the nape of my neck. I don't know what I'm doing, but I do know his kiss feels like home.

We sit out under the willow until the sun rises. Trading kisses and talking about everything. He wants to know it all. When the first rays of dawn cut through, he helps me to my feet and we walk back together, hand in hand.

Nothing was ever the same.

CHAPTER SEVEN
Dean

I sit in my truck outside the bar, nursing my third cup of coffee since dropping Donnie back at the Saints. He's texted me a few times, checking in. I don't have an update for him. Just reiterating I'm not moving until I know where she's living. From there, well I don't really have a plan. Only a desperate need to check out her house, to make sure it's in a safe area, somewhere I can watch things, or remove her if necessary.

Is it stalkerish? Yes.

Do I care? That's a resounding no.

Being this close to her and doing nothing is driving me crazy. When 2am rolls around, a small car pulls to the curb, sitting idle. The server from earlier climbs out of the driver's seat and helps finagle a *very* intoxicated Sage and a giggling Tessalynn into the back seat. There's a man at the door locking things up, when he turns around, I recognize him as one of the bartenders. Shifting my eyes to the car, I watch as the server digs into Sage's pockets, pulling out a set of keys and tossing them to the man. He waves daintily at the drunken fools before blowing them each a kiss.

Ohhhhkay, so not a boyfriend.

He walks around the building and a few moments later, a sage green –because of course it's sage green- Toyota Tacoma pulls in front of the black car. The man seems to be playing captain of this shit show. I wait a few moments, until I see the server's car turn right at the end of the intersection before pulling out and following. It's late. Not many travelers on the road. It's not hard to stay far enough back and follow without garnering suspicion.

They drive for about 20 minutes before pulling into a cookie cutter residential area. Each house is in a nice little row, with small garages attached. I hang back, it won't be hard to figure out where they went. Pulling to an intersection with a good view of the houses on this street, I look for which one they stop at. Shutting off my own vehicle, I roll my windows down to listen. The Toyota pulls into the driveway first. The house they're at is cute, in a very suburbia kind of way. From here I can see the white siding and the freshly mowed lawn.

This is where she lives?

The man hops out of the truck and charges to the car, barely catching a falling Tessalynn as she stumbles from the back seat. For a moment, I'm concerned as she gulps a giant lungful of air and bends over, hands to her knees. It's then I realize she's gagging. The man groans so loudly, I can hear him from here. He waves his hands in front of his face in disgust before squaring his shoulders and pulling Sage from the vehicle and leans her carefully against it. The server comes around the car and passes him something that looks like baby wipes. I can hear Tessalynn rambling, but it's in Spanish and she's going way too fast for me to comprehend. Then the server grabs Tessalynn by the shoulders and starts guiding her to the front door, once on the porch she digs a key from her purse, and they enter.

Of course she has a key. I know this isn't her place because Jora sent me her file while I waited, she lives 20 minutes in the opposite direction. But what really piques my curiosity is the fact Tessalynn's file was vague, *enough so* that I'll have Donnie take a deeper dive at some point. I return my attention back to Sage; she's apologizing profusely, and the bartender just shakes his head as he wipes her face. Then he lifts her effortlessly in his arms.

Jealousy turns my stomach. Deep down, I know it's a harmless act, a friend helping her get to bed quicker. If I thought he had nefarious intentions, I'd march over there, but something tells me he's not interested like that. The server holds the door open for them and they too disappear into the house. Roughly ten minutes later, both the server and the bartender came back out. Before they get in the black car, they roll all the windows down.

Then it dawns on me, *my girl can't hold her liquor.*

Finally understanding all the fuss, I bark a loud laugh into the empty truck. When they pull away, I wait a few more minutes for the lights in the house to shut off before getting out and doing a perimeter check.

Walking closer, I shake my head, tsking, when I notice the security system sign in her yard.

That's a terrible idea sweetheart, you're just advertising how easy it'll be for someone skilled to break through.

Walking the length of the privacy fence, I'm momentarily irritated by the locked gate, even though it's smart of her. Not deterred, I inch up slightly and peer over. I'm standing at 6'4", so it's easy to see the back yard. The first thing I notice is that there's no ornamentation. Just a push mower tucked in a corner and a small concrete patio, with a fire pit off to the side and no chairs.

Does she not use the space? That doesn't sound right. Sage loves being outdoors.

Making my way back to the front, I find the garage open at the bottom. Bending low, I army crawl closer to the edge, if anyone drives by and sees me, they're going to call the police. I need to make this quick. Pulling my phone from my pocket, I use the flashlight to look at what she's keeping in here. I'm starving for information. On the left side of the room, there are cardboard boxes stacked in a neat row, swiveling the light to the other side, I see a treadmill, and some broken down boxes. Nothing else. Did she just move in? Or is she moving out? These are simple questions I wish I had the answers to.

Popping up, I make my way back to my truck, sending a text to my brother as I go, letting him know what I've discovered. With nothing left to do, I need to head back to the clubhouse and get a few hours of sleep before meeting with Petey. We know the Russians are here, we know they're frequenting the bar. But what we don't know is why. If I had to guess, based on the little I know so far, it has something to do with Sage. The reasoning doesn't fit. Jora was right.

I fucking hate missing puzzle pieces too.

CHAPTER EIGHT
Sage

I hate her, I truly do. After Tessa strong armed me into singing, she shoved shot after shot in my face. I've never regretted meeting her more than I do in this moment. I vaguely remember getting home. When I opened my eyes this morning, vomit was imminent. My head was pounding as I crawled (and I do mean this literally), I fucking crawled to the ensuite. My legs wouldn't cooperate. I hugged that porcelain throne and purged the last 25 years' worth of liquid I've ever consumed into the bowl, like some sort of sick offering to the toilet gods.

Oh, I fucking hate her.

As I lay on my bathroom floor, contemplating all my life choices, a cool washcloth draped over my eyes, Tessa bounds in, with an inhuman pep in her step and a grin on her stupid fucking face. When she snatches the rag, I hiss at her like a feral cat. Ignoring me with an eyeroll, she holds a steaming cup of caffeinated gold above my face. Lazily, I lift my arms grasping at the mug, trying to breathe in its essence. When those first notes of coffee hit my nostrils, I'm already feeling more alive than I did. As I lean up gingerly, taking a sip, she nudges my lips, so I keep my mouth open as she drops two Tylenol down the hatch without saying a word, after that something plops down beside me. I'm still mad, I'm still pouting. This is the hangover of all hangovers. When I glance down, wincing, -*fast move bad, slow move good-*...I see it's a fucking banana. Without waiting for me to ask why, she answers my unspoken question.

"Bananas are good for hangovers. Drink your coffee, eat your banana. Wash your ass and por el amor de Dios, brush your teeth mami. Then meet me in the living room."

"So, bossy." I grumble.

"You know it babe." She winks and flounces away, taking all the audacity with her.

Hurricane. Fucking. Tessa.

God, I love her.

25 minutes later and I'm dragging ass into the living room. The smells coming from my kitchen are heavenly. Did I mention I love her? She sings something softly to herself in Spanish while whisking eggs. There's bacon sizzling in another pan, I lean against the island as I watch her refill her coffee mug, she picks up a bottle of Bailey's Irish cream before pouring a generous amount into her coffee as creamer. I'm beginning to understand why she's not feeling it like I am, hair of the dog does a girl wonders I suppose. When she notices me, she grins saucily and offers me the bottle. I just shake my head 'no' and she shrugs irreverently, returning to what she's doing.

I ask, "How did we get home?"

While cooking, she says, "Antony and Nikki. Your truck is in the driveway in case you were wondering?"

"Who drove my truck?"

"Antony did, Nikki drove us. She gave him a ride home after they dropped us off here." She turns around, a nervous smile on her face, "By the way, you puked in Nikki's car."

I slap a palm over my face with a groan. "I didn't really, did I?"

She pats my arm sympathetically, "You did cariña, but fear not, I offered to take care of the detailing. It was my idea to bring you out and I did get you to go a tiny bit overboard."

"A tiny bit?" I ask incredulously.

She pinches her thumb and index finger together, holding them so very close. "Just a tiny bit. No es mi culpa que seas un peso ligero!"

"I'm not a lightweight Tessie. You seem to forget; we played quarters, and that one guy bought me a drink without you."

She plates her food as she asks, "So what happened with him? He looked like he'd be a good time. He had the swagger."

"The swagger?" I ask, before popping a piece of bacon in my mouth. It's so good, I moan.

"Si, energía de la polla grande." She sits at my small dining table and gestures for me to join her. I threw a few pieces of bacon on a plate and a generous helping of eggs. She made them nice and fluffy, with just a sprinkling of tajin. Settling in with my breakfast, I eat quietly for a minute before addressing her statement.

"I suppose he did have that sort of vibe. I mean, yes, he was nice to look at. But there was something predatory about the way he smiled at me. He looked like he wanted to eat me."

She waves her fork in my face and rolls her eyes, "Harlow. You should have LET THE MAN EAT YOU! How many times do I have to say it, you need a good roll in bed. You're wound too tight. All this stress, with no real release is going to kill you before anyone else does."

She winces at my reaction to that last bit. "Too much?"

"Gee, I don't know Tess. You tell me." I glared at her unimpressed.

Sighing forcefully, she says "Lo siento, hermana. I didn't mean it. I just worry about you. You hold yourself back from life."

Before I can dive into this, there's a knock on my door. It's 10am on a Tuesday, UPS doesn't usually deliver this early. Tess arches a brow at me, "Are you expecting a package?"

I shake my head, "Unless you sent something here, no, I just moved in Tess. I haven't even updated my prime address."

We eye each other for just a moment before she motions with both hands for me to stay in my seat and heads to the front door. After a few minutes, she still hadn't returned. Gingerly I make my way to her, when I hit round the corner I see a bouquet of flowers in her arms. Not just any flowers. Black roses.

I catch sight of a white card clenched in her fist, "What does it say?"

She shakes her head. It's the first time I've ever seen her at a loss for words. She looks at me, holding the wrapped bundle tightly to her chest. Her eyes are wide, pleading, the color drained from her golden skin. Reaching out slowly, she grabs my hand, steadying it. I hadn't realized I started shaking. I'm frozen for just a beat before I move.

My cell phone is in my bedroom. Rushing through my home, Tessa's hot on my heels. Ripping my cell from the charger I find Brad's number and hit dial. The line rings once, twice, three times before he answers.

"Harlow, how's it goin?" He sounds entirely too chipper for me.

"Hey Brad, how's Jeri, she doing ok?" I'm trying to keep the tremble from my voice, but it's not working. He notices it.

"She's good, are you okay?" I don't have the mental capacity for his concern right now.

"I'm fine. Just missing her. Nothing amiss?" I ask, biting my thumbnail.

"No, everything's good here. The girls are eating breakfast now before we start morning drills. Want me to grab her, let you check in?"

If I talk to Jericho, she'll notice I'm off. I could play it down as missing her, but I don't want to do that. She should enjoy being a kid for as long as she can. Warring with myself, I decide to let it be for now, give myself time to think.

"No, no. Just wanted to check in. Don't interrupt her, she'll think I'm lame." I muster up a laugh I'm not feeling.

Brad chuckles too, not catching my vibe. Which is preferable to be honest.

"Well, I'll call you if anything comes up. But for now, I ought to get back at it." His voice drops while he adds, "If you ever need to talk, I'm here. I know what you said, I'm here as a friend Harlow."

Brad really is a sweet man. But I don't want sweet. I don't want a man. Not if I can't have the one I really want. I'm not going to get into all that, thanking him, I end the call. Tessa has planted herself on my bed, in a daze, she's still holding the flowers. When I go to grab them from, she twists away, pulling them with her. Her face is anguished, pleading. Taking a step back, I dropped my hand, confused.

"What was on the note?" I'm almost afraid to ask. The jovial Tessa is gone, her face twists with rage.

"No." giving one imperceptible shake.

"What did it say?" She shakes her head again, lower lip trembling.

"I'm sorry for what I said earlier, I want you to know that. I love you and I love Jericho." the damn breaks and the tears flow, in gasping breaths she continues, "I don't want you to read it. I don't want you to have to leave."

I don't hesitate to reach out and pull her into my arms. We sit huddled together on my bed for what feels like an eternity before she sits back up and wipes her face. She levels me with a look, biting down on her lip. "You need to talk to big brother."

Oh, fuck me running.

I didn't even think about Thorne during this. Being shitfaced as I was last night, I know for a fact I didn't check the burner cell. Lunging across the bed, I pull it from the drawer, holding my breath as I wait for it to power on. Tessa is hovering over my shoulder while the barrage of messages come through. I look at her, I'm scared. I know she is too. When I open the one and only thread, there are seven texts.

Thorne: Not safe.

Thorne: I'm handling it.

Thorne: Don't move.

Thorne: I'm coming to you.

Thorne: I mean it Sage. DO NOT RUN. Stay put.

Thorne: I love you sis.

Thorne: You should know, Dean's in NOLA.

I read the messages over and over while pacing across my bedroom floor. Dean is in New Orleans? When I turn back to Tessa, her eyes are flitting all over my face, mouth covered by her hands. She's as shocked as I am. There are black spots dancing in my vision. When I go to take a breath, *fuck I've been holding it this whole time*, it's too late. The last thing I see before I crumple is Tessa's face as she lunges for me.

CHAPTER NINE
Dean

When I pull through the gate, I nod my head at the prospect on duty. I'm bone tired. It's been the longest day of my life, not to mention the emotional fuckery weighing on me. I need to push it back. The day when it can be addressed will come. For now, I've got other things to worry about. I'll keep Sage safe, then I'll unleash my wrath for the lie.

I'm angry. So. Fucking. Angry.

Thorne isn't off the hook for this, not by a long shot. There's a reason I'm the club fixer. I stay cool under pressure, but when I unleash the inner demon, problems don't just stop, they disappear completely. No person, no problem. For the sake of getting by, I need to reprogram my mindset, push the darkness down. If I lose control now, there's no telling what I'll do.

Donnie's asleep when I let myself back into the guest cottage. Once in the bathroom, I start the shower. Undressing, I catch my reflection in the mirror. Homing in on my neck, I still remember the day I got the tattoo. It would have been Sage's 21st birthday. What was she doing then? Did she celebrate? Alive and vibrant and so fucking far away. I shake my head and climb under the spray, replaying the events of the night. She looked good, so fucking good tonight. Fuck me if she didn't come into herself. Those tight jeans, the banded top.

I've got my hand around my dick in an instant, squeezing hard along my shaft, fucking my hand to thoughts of her. Just like every time I do this, it's her I see. Only her. Right now, I'm picturing her on stage with nothing but the guitar for coverage. Her raspy voice, singing that song again. I'd approach her this time, slip my hands up her lean legs and find that spot I've been missing. I'd reduce her to ashes, the same way she's done me. Gripping myself harder, I pump my fist faster, images of her filter in like a slideshow. I imagine she's in here with me, a small hand wrapped around my dick, intertwined with mine. Guiding her as she brings me to climax. I'd twist her copper curls around my fist and bare her throat before biting down. Slamming her into the wall, I'd pound into her from behind. I'd leave my mark for all to see. That does it, with a groan I cum, milky ropes shoot across the shower walls.

It didn't make me feel any better, the opposite in fact.

I crave more.

Dissatisfied with myself and the situation, I finish my shower quickly and climb into bed.

It feels like I've just closed my eyes when a shift in the air wakes me. I'm reaching under the pillow for my pistol when I hear slurping. I crack an eye and see Donnie leaning against the door frame. Cup of coffee held to his mouth; one hand tucked in his pocket he stands there with an amused expression on his face.

"What time is it?" My voice is raspy from sleep.

"It's 11am sunshine. You going to sleep all day?"

I fling a pillow that he easily dodges. My heart wasn't in it anyhow. "Fuck you Donal."

"Ouch, you wound me brother, here I was coming to give you a positive start to your morning. Have my bright face be the first one you see." He brings his hand to his heart dramatically. As I ease up into a sitting position, I ignore him and tilt my head towards the mug in his hand, "There anymore of that?"

"There is. Would you like some?" he asks with a playful smile.

"Yeah. I would."

He snickers before kicking off the wall, "Then go make yourself a cup." He's scrambling away with a laugh as the next pillow flies.

I drag myself up and into the bathroom to take care of my morning business. I'd just finished pulling my cut on over a black tee when Donnie walks back into the room with a thermos outstretched, handing it to me.

I smirk at him, "You love me, you really love me."

He laughs dryly, "Nah, I just know how you are without this shit in the morning, and I don't want to subject baby Petey to it." I clap him on the back and bark out a laugh. As we make our way to the clubhouse proper, I notice the guys that were partying last night look a bit more put together today. Don nudges me with his elbow, "You never mentioned how you knew Petey."

Shrugging, I keep it vague.

"I met him down in Texas about a year ago, at the Saint's club there. Gave him some pointers."

Truth is, Petey got caught up with the Cartel and I saved his ass. It's his story to tell though, so I'm not going to dive too deep.

Donnie eyes me skeptically, but he knows that's all he's getting from me. There are too many other things on my mind.

Dropping it for the time being, we head into church.

When church is over, I'm happier than when we first got here. Petey isn't the fool I took him for initially. He has a plan in place for the Bratva visitors, already safeguarding the weapons and blow stashed at various warehouses in the area. We go over what we know and what Colin's expectations are as far as bloodshed.

Minimal, if possible. Don't start a fight but be prepared to finish one.

He has no wife and no known heir to his animal kingdom. No desire for war unless Medvedev makes the first move. The Saints ride with Colin, so his will be done. I pull Petey aside and ask for a protection detail in Sage's neighborhood, giving him as little information as possible, he doesn't hesitate and offers to put a few guys on a rotating shift. It's one of the things I've come to appreciate about him. He's a 'go with the flow kind' of dude. You can tell he's listening and calculating everything, putting his trust in us until I give him a reason not to.

I'd just stepped outside, intending on riding for a bit to clear my head when my cell phone rang. It's Jora.

"Hey man, what have you got?" I ask while sitting on my bike.

"Issues."

Barking out a laugh, I muse "Tell me something I don't know."

"The friend called Thorne."

His tone catches my attention, "That something new?"

"According to Thorne, yeah it is. He never talks to Tess directly."

"It's Tess now?" I can practically hear his eyes rolling as he snipes back at me.

"Tessalynn is a mouthful."

I'm sitting on my bike, kicking pieces of gravel with the toe of my boot, "What did Tess have to say?"

He's quiet for a moment, "I need you to remain calm. Can you do that?"

I clench the phone tighter in my grip. "I'm the picture of calm."

Lie.

"Your sarcasm could use some work my friend."

I grit my teeth, proving him right as I lose my patience, "Jora, get to the point."

"Right, Tess, they're best friends by the way -she made sure to tell me several times- called from the burner Thorne gave Sage. Apparently, she'd received some sort of threat. In the form of black roses, she passed out shortly after and instead of calling the police –I like her by the way- she calls big brother."

"You talked to her?"

He laughs, "Of course, I had to introduce myself obviously. She's a wildcat."

Catching Donnie as he's coming out of the clubhouse; I lift my free hand and motion for him to get on his bike. Focusing back on Jora, I ask, "How long ago was this?"

The phone muffles for a second before Thorne comes on the line. "It was about 30 minutes ago. Sage's been out for the last ten, she's just sleeping. I walked Tess through checking her pulse. Just in case. She said they drank quite a bit last night, more than Sage typically does. So, I'm thinking the hangover combined with the stress knocked her out. Tess is going to let her sleep, but I told her not to go anywhere." he pauses before sighing, "She's expecting you, but she won't make it easy."

"Awesome, looking forward to it. We'll head her way in a moment."

"We?" he asks.

"Me and Don." I'm running my fingers over the handlebars, itching with impatience.

"That's probably smart, Tess can be a handful on a good day." Blowing out a ragged breath, he says, "There's something else you should know."

"If you're about to drop another bomb on me, I'll shoot you on sight."

"I guess you're shooting me." He laughs mirthlessly.

"What now Thorne?" I ask, sighing with resignation.

"She has a little girl."

My heart picks up, "Who has a little girl?"

"It's not the way I imagine she'd want you to find out." I detect a hint of pity in his tone, and my hackles rise immediately. "Sage has a daughter; you need to know."

"Stop." My stomach bottoms out, I'm not sure if I'm breathing. The pain in my chest is sudden, borderline excruciating.

Is this what it feels like to have a heart attack?

"Her name is Jericho. I'm only telling you about her because the threat was addressed specifically to her. There was a card, her name was mentioned. I'm following up with one of my CI's and heading your way at the end of the week. Can I trust you to look after my sister and niece, Dean?"

My mind spins with all the shit that's been dumped on me in the last 24 hours. The question though, can he trust me?

Obviously, more than I can ever trust him again.

She wasn't pregnant before the barn burned; I would have known.

Unless it's not mine. Unless she left me for someone else.

Then there's the fact that Thorne didn't call her my daughter, he warned me, he pitied me… asked me to look after his niece.

Not my daughter.

Struggling to clear my throat, I reassure him. "Yeah. I won't let anything happen either of them."

"That's what I'm counting on." he says cryptically and ends the call before I do.

Starting my bike in a daze, I walk it backwards so I can pull out. Donnie does the same. Before we take off, he reaches out clasping a hand on my shoulder. Concern written in the furrow of his brow. "Are you good?" he yells over the rumbling.

I nod absentmindedly, I'm not good. I'm the furthest from good there's ever been. But I have a job to do. I'll protect her and the girl. Then I'll ride away. Like I was never here at all. That's the smart move, then... I'll move on.

"Let's go." I yelled back, pulling out.

It takes about an hour to make it to Sage's house. The closer I get, the clearer I can see Tessa standing on the porch, arms crossed over her chest. She looks like she's gearing up for a fight. Fuck all that, Don can handle this one.

After parking in her driveway, I waited on my Harley for Don to do the same beside me. I hunch forward and cross my arms over the handlebars as my brother stands from his bike. When I make no move to get up, he reads my intentions and makes his way over to her. He's two steps from the porch when she squares her shoulders and narrows her eyes at him. Too fast for me to make out, she's rapid firing in Spanish.

"Antes de que des un paso más, déjame decirte algo. No miento cuando digo que sé cómo despellejar a un hombre. Si quieres lastimar a mis chicas. ¡Ve ahora, si es así!"

Clearly, Donnie has a better understanding than I do, as she speaks, his face goes from affectionate, to shocked, then pure awe. When she finishes, he looks at me, with a reassuring smile before relaxing his stance. He tucks one hand in his pocket, going for nonchalance and answers her –much to my surprise- in fluent Spanish.

"Sé que hablas inglés, pero esto es más divertido. No tiene ni idea de lo que has dicho. Creo que eso es bueno. Si mi hermano supiera que nos amenazaste, sacaría una pistola." her jaw drops, "Preferiría no apuntar con un arma a la mujer con la que planeo casarme." she growls at that and he winks at her before continuing somberly. "Somos amables. Lo prometo. Sage es muy importante para él". He pauses, looking at me briefly before returning his attention back to her. "Se arrancaría el corazón antes de lastimar a Sage."

She waves him away, snapping. "Enough. Who sent you?"

The look she's giving him would cut a lesser man down, not Donnie. He smiles at her, all teeth, daring her to show him what she's got. I've never seen him look so invigorated.

I answer from my bike, "Thorne."

Without another word, she goes through the front door, I'm expecting her to slam it in our faces, but instead she holds it open and ushers us inside.

I take a deep breath before following my brother across the threshold. I feel out of place in my dusty boots and ripped jeans. Needing to do something with my hands, I pull the elastic off my wrist and pull my hair into a bun. I pause in the living area, afraid to sit down. This moment is surreal. I'm back in her space for the first time in years and I don't know what to do with myself. I take in the hardwood floors and sandstone painted walls. It's an open floor plan with a hallway leading to what I assume are bedrooms and bathroom. To my left there's a small sectional and coffee table. A decent television is mounted on the wall. Across from the sofa is a large bookshelf, home to a vast collection. A few steps and I'm running my fingers across their spines. Sage always did love reading about other places. Getting lost and escaping reality. Tearing my gaze from there, I note there are no photos. Nothing personal on display. It's simple and clean. The room smells of lemongrass and vanilla. It gives my theory that she's just moved in merit.

Returning my attention to my brother, I see Donnie and the hellcat have moved to the dining nook. She offers him a cup of coffee before settling down at the table to sip on her own. We both watch as she pulls a small bottle of Jameson from her pocket and dumps half of it into her mug.

Catching our stares, she grimaces. "It's been a stressful day. I need a little something to take the edge off." After bringing the mug to her lips, she looked between the both of us chewing on her bottom lip.

"Don't do that darlin', you'll ruin those perfect lips before I have a chance to taste them." She cuts her gaze at my brother, snarling in disgust. With a lazy shrug, he tips his own mug and smiles. He's really enjoying himself.

"Cerdo." She coughs under her breath. Rolling my eyes at the two of them, I interrupt Don's laughter with a question.

"What exactly happened today?" She sets her mug down shakily and stares into it. My brother moves closer to... comfort? I'm not sure. With a harsh shake of my head, he stops in his tracks. This isn't time to play white knight. We need answers. He sobers and stays standing sentry against the kitchen counter.

Tessa looks up at me with tired eyes and asks, "Who are you? Thorne just said someone was coming to help. To protect the girls. So, who are you?" She nudges her thumb in Don's direction. "Why would the brute say you'd cut your own heart out for my friend?"

Donnie looks at me, shrugging with an apology. The truth is, I don't know how to answer anymore. Before I have a chance to really dive into it, the most beautiful sound interrupts me.

"Hello Raven."

CHAPTER TEN
Sage, Age 16

I'm dreaming. I must be. I'm walking down a long hallway covered in glass, droplets of blood scattered around. I've been here before. There's a door at the end of the hallway. An ethereal glow illuminating the frame. If I can make it to the door, I can finally see what's been waiting for me. My steps falter, I don't want to know. I don't want to go to the door. I stop. Turning around, I see Dean. He smiles at me and offers a hand. I step into his embrace. He smells of sandalwood and leather. I love it. I love him. I've never said it. But I do. He holds me tight, leaning down so his lips are at my ear and whispers, "You were never meant to be mine." I pulled back, confused. He speaks again, but I can't hear him. He glances over my shoulder in a panic, he starts yelling, but no sound touches my ears. There's a tugging sensation in my gut, I'm pulled from him. I reach out at the same time he does, just as our fingers are about to touch, I'm yanked again.

Then I wake up.

Light from the hall slices through my room. Thorne is at basic training and Fern is at church camp. I've been left to deal with Hattie on my own. My bedroom door is cracked, I'm positive I shut and locked it before bed. Sometimes Dean creeps up my balcony for a sleep over, I'd never have not locked my door, just in case Hattie decided to be nosey. That would be a nightmare. It wouldn't matter to her that we haven't gone all the way yet; she wouldn't understand I love having him close to me. The voices grow louder. It's a man, his voice heavily accented. Hattie yells louder and the sound of glass breaking sends me scrambling towards my door. As I go to shut it, my name drifts up the staircase, I hesitate. Doorknob in hand, I listen.

"I need the money now." Hattie slurs. The man says something in a language I'm not familiar with. It's throaty, guttural. Something about his tone makes me nervous. I don't have to be fluent to know he's angry. "We've given. You get what you need for now. Boss says stop hitting girl." Something slams again and I don't want to be here anymore.

A quick check of the phone Dean gave me tells me it's only a little after midnight. I have no indication he's coming tonight, but I close my door quietly and shoot him a text anyway.

Songbird: I'm going to the tree.

A few moments later, he responds.

Raven: Now?

Songbird: Yes.

Raven: Alright. I was wrapping something up for Pops. I'll be there. Stay in the shadows baby. See you soon.

After shimmying into a pair of gym shorts, I decided to leave my sleep shirt on, figuring I can get a rise out of Dean when he sees I still have his senior football tee, after a day of swimming, he let me borrow it and I refused to give it back. On the nights he can't come, it brings comfort. Pulling my flip flops from under the bed, I step into them while making my way to my bedroom balcony and use the lattice to climb down. Once my feet hit the grass, I slip the shoes back off and hang them from my fingers as I hightail it to the tree. Running cross country for Ravenswood High makes this little trek easy. Once I'm under the willow's coverage, I climb up onto my preferred branch and wait. Spring air makes the branches sway in the balmy breeze. Sitting back, I close my eyes and listen to the locust's song. An hour later, I've got my knees pulled to my chest when I see Dean break through the wisps. He strolls casually to me, smiling up at my perched position. I relax, letting one leg dangle in front of him and speak softly, "Hello Raven."

He grins mischievously before running one calloused hand up the back of my calf and wrapping it around my thigh. When he starts to massage the muscle, I groan. He pauses briefly, looking up at me, his eyes are dark, pupils blown. Reaching up, he drags my other leg down too. Both dangle on each side of his shoulders. Dean's grown to a towering height in the last year. Just over six feet. Once he has both of my legs where he wants them, he cups my ass and pulls me down so I'm hugging his waist. Squealing in delight, I lock my ankles around his back, clinging to him like a monkey while he finds a good spot and sits with me in his lap.

Smiling down at him, I find he's staring up at me in wonder. "I'll never get tired of this you know?"

"Get tired of what?" I mumble back.

"You."

Relaxing into him, I run my fingers through his black hair, then move down to caress his back, my hands roaming anywhere I can touch. I'll never get tired of him either.

Leaning in, he starts working his mouth from my jaw to my collarbones, running his tongue across my clavicle slowly. The shirt is large and the neckline gapes. Taking advantage of that, he tugs it to the side and places small bites on my shoulder. Kissing the hurt away each time. Moving up, he finally reaches my lips and I'm a goner. Under the tree, we trade kisses for a little while, then he pulls back, resting his forehead against mine.

He whispers softly, "I love you Songbird." My breath catches in my throat, but he keeps going, like if he doesn't say it all now, he'll never get it out. "I have loved you since the first moment I saw you, I didn't even know what love was, but I knew that the way I felt for you was powerful. So powerful I wasn't sure how to handle it until you put me out of my misery." He laughs, "I love you so fucking much Sage."

Tears fall from my lashes; as he reaches his thumb up to brush them away, I stop him. Grabbing his hand, I place it over my chest and keep it there. I ask him, "You feel that? My heart beats for you. Steadily strumming, like a song. I'll always be yours, have been from day one. I love you too Dean."

Crushing me to him, he kisses my forehead, my nose and then lips. I curl into his chest and just breathe. He wraps his arms around me.

I'm safe. I'm home.

Finally realizing I left the house first instead of waiting for him, he asks me in a low rumble, "Did something happen?"

I should mention the man, but I know once I do, Dean will insist on checking it out. If he finds something he doesn't like, he'll lose his temper. This is too nice to ruin. We've just owned our feelings, and I want to bask in it. Deciding to keep it to myself, I go with a partial truth. "Hattie's just drunk again. She woke me up. Needed to escape for a bit."

Leaning in, he kisses my forehead again, lips staying pressed to my skin as he murmurs, "Want to come home with me? Think she'll notice?"

"I don't care if she does. Let's go." I lift off his lap without hesitation and wiggle my fingers for him to take my hand. He smiles as he does, and together, we venture off into the night.

Later, as we were tangled in his bed, I gave myself to him in a different way.

Completely and wholly. He had me, mind, body and soul.

CHAPTER ELEVEN
Sage

I wake abruptly to the sounds of yelling. Straining my ears, I figured out it was Tessa yelling. Pieces of the day trickle back in through the residual fog of sleep. After wiping my eyes, I grab a bat from behind my bedroom door and tiptoe into the hall. Thanks to my brother, I know to keep my stance loose, at the ready. No one is in the house. Standing on the porch my girl is on a tirade. When she finally finishes her threatening speech, a deep voice replies to her saucily.

God he really likes her sort of crazy.

The longer I listen, I realize the stranger's deep drawl is familiar. Jumping a few times and rolling my shoulders, I'm preparing to charge onto the porch -literally go up to bat- when I heard him.

After Tess asked who sent them, the rumbled, 'Thorne' almost brings me to my knees.

He's here.

I knew that voice in the depths of my being. Had heard it in every form possible. My face heats as I recall hearing it moan out my name in the throes of pleasure.

What is wrong with you? Now is not the time for this.

He's here. He's here. He's here.

My brother must have given him our location. But why? Before I could process what this meant, Tess stormed through the front door. With wide eyes, she stops abruptly at the threshold, one arm on the front door and considers my position at the end of the hall. Mouthing 'Go!'. She shakes her head and shoos me vehemently back to my room. I'd only just made it back to the hallway when the sound of boots hit the hardwood floors. Two sets. The first followed Tess into the dining nook, but the second, they walked into the living room and just stopped.

Dean was in my home, in my living room, breathing in my air. If the muffled movement was an indicator, he was also checking out my lack of things. Like a static charge broadcasting his presence I could feel him. He couldn't have been more than six feet away from my hiding place. Pressing flat against the wall, I try to regulate my breathing. This wasn't how I'd pictured a reunion.

Really, I'd never given myself hope of having one.

Knowing he was here, so close to me, I wasn't sure what to do. This wasn't an ideal position for box breathing, sittings better, but I needed to calm down. With my feet firmly planted on the floor, I straightened to my full height, relaxing my hands at my side. I exhaled all the air in my lungs, before breathing in for a four count and then exhaling the same way. This usually worked when the panic got too high. After four rotations, I felt more in control. I could do this.

Everyone had moved to the dining nook. I ran my hands through my curls slowly, fixing any unruly bits. Not that it really mattered I suppose. He'll either be happy to see me or he won't. As I round the corner, I hear Tessa. "Why would the brute say you'd cut your own heart out for my friend?"

My steps are silent as I walk towards them. Before Dean has a chance to respond. I speak. "Hello Raven."

His back is to me as I enter the room, at the sound of my voice, every muscle in his delectable body turns rigid in response. Time seems to stand still as he slowly rotates. On the outside, I'm calm, but on the inside, I'm frothing like the tumultuous sea. I watch every sinew and muscle shift on his corded forearms as he tightens his fists.

I didn't realize forearms could be so sexy.

Grey eyes meet mine, unable to help myself, I take him in. The man is a walking canvas. Tattoos flow from his fingers, winding a path up his arms, they're beautiful. I take in the VP patch on his vest and shift my gaze towards his bearded face. He's so tan, as if he's spent all his days on the back of his bike. Full lips part slightly, and those silver eyes are wide with shock. A black hoop sits on the side of his straight nose. He's sex on a stick. Oozing primal masculinity.

Dean Graham ladies and gentlemen. All. Fucking. Man.

The lean boy I knew is gone, he towers over me, imposing. The chest on this guy, oh how I'd love to feel the weight of it on top of me. When I catch his scent, my eyes flutter involuntarily and my nostrils flare, it's taking everything in me to hold back a moan.

God, I've missed him.

He still smells of leather, mint and just a hint of sandalwood. It's enough to make heat coil in my lower belly and my mouth water.

It's too much, like staring at the sun. I wasn't expecting it. I wasn't expecting him. This morning was stressful enough, it seems like today is a gift that keeps on giving. Tears pool in my eyes and I'm struggling to blink them away. One breaks free and his thumb is there, catching it. He looks at me affectionately before he drawls softly, "Hello Songbird."

Quickly as it appeared, the affection is replaced with a hardness as he seems to remember the last eight years, what I've done. His face shutters and he shuts down. Those silver eyes are burning while his perfect jaw clenches.

We lost ourselves for a moment.

The cold reality check of our situation punches me in the face, and I ask quietly, "What are you doing here?"

Through gritted teeth, "Thorne sent us to look after you. He told us about the threat to you and your daughter."

My head rears back. Your daughter? I look at Tessa questioningly. She shakes her head sadly and holds up the card she refused to show me earlier. I cross the room in three quick strides and snatch it from her outstretched hand. "I'm sorry mami, I couldn't bring myself to show it to you. But you do need to know."

Written in an elegant script, 'The walls of Jericho fell, so will you. I'm coming to collect what's due'.

Through clenched teeth, I grit out, "Tess, you should have told me. I would have gone to get her. We could be on our way back by now." I'm pissed and she knows it. Giving me a sheepish look for a moment before casting her eyes down in shame. It's not very often I lose my temper, especially with her.

Mulling it over, I realize Dean doesn't seem to know Jericho is his daughter. Big brother must not have shown all my cards. If he did, this conversation would be going quite differently. Setting the message gently on the table I recall there were two people who entered my home. Turning to my left, I see him, the owner of the other voice. Donnie leans against my kitchen counter, patiently sipping coffee. When he sees I've finally noticed him, his mouth breaks out in the biggest shit eating grin. Setting his mug down on the counter, my old friend closes the distance and lifts me into a bear hug. Behind us, there's a deep growl and

Tessa's cackle.

Donnie holds me tight, whispering in my ear, "Don't leave again."

I whisper back, "I may not have a choice." Donnie holds me at arm's length, with a wink and mischievous grin over my shoulder, he whispers back, "We'll see." then he says loudly, "Damn you filled out in all the right places Songbird."

There's a sigh before a throat clears pointedly, "Donal, if you're done?"

Don's still looking at me, eyes soft, "I've missed you darlin'."

Emotion strangles my throat, "I've missed you too."

Dean scoffs and walks to my living room, the dismissal clear. Donnie lets me go to follow. Tessa catches my eye; the apprehension is clear. She should have told me. We'll be discussing this later, of that I'm sure. She rises from her seat and takes my hand, squaring my shoulders, I let her and together we join them. Tessa sits on the sectional facing Dean, tugging me down beside her. Off to the side, Don is snooping through my bookshelf, momentarily distracting me. He laughs when he pulls down a copy of 'Goodnight Moon', flipping through the pages. "Mom used to read this to us, remember D?"

Dean doesn't answer him, granite eyes on me, like he can't believe I'm real. For just a moment, I see something that looks like anguish in his piercing gaze, it's brief but it's there. Then he puts the mask back on and levels me with a dark expression. "Where's your daughter?"

"She's at camp until the end of the week."

I drop my head before answering, I can't look at him. If I do, I'll break down and beg for his forgiveness. Finding my hands very fascinating at the moment, I pick at my cuticles. I'm waiting for the other shoe to drop; like a ticking time bomb.

Unaware of my inner turmoil, Dean continues, "You should probably get her back earlier than planned. That way I can keep an eye on the both of you in one place."

That snaps me out of it. "Keep an eye on us? As in here?"

He rolls his eyes and then narrows them at me, snarling, "Do you have a problem with me staying here?"

And there's the other shoe.

Fuck yeah, I've got a problem with it.

This is so complicated. Everything I was afraid of happening is fucking happening. They'll use her against me. There's so much to unpack. I don't want her involved; I've never wanted her to know about any of this. She needs to enjoy being a child. I swore to protect her and it's clear I'm failing miserably. Have I been deluding myself this whole time? This is my fault. I got complacent, never should have stepped on the stage and out of the shadows.

"Dios mío, give her a minute," Tessa rubs my shoulders, before muttering under her breath, "hombre estúpido."

She lifts my chin, so we're eye level, communicating without words. Her eyes are telling me to *do the right thing, it's time to tell the truth.* I give her pained look back as if to say *I can't,* her face hardens, brow furrowing, as if to say *yes bitch you can and you need to, he's her father and it's clear he wants to protect you.* Do it for her. After an intense stare off, I break first and nod my head in resignation. Letting go of me, she looks entirely too pleased with herself. Dean will probably never forgive me, I'm not expecting it, I only need him to understand. But if we're going to do this, we're going to do it my way.

Hugging my friend, I ask her to stay for a while, then turn to Donnie and ask, "Will you stay with her? Me and the big man need to take a drive." He looks surprised by my request, both of us turning to Dean.

Indifferently, he approves the request with a wave of his tattooed hand.

"Yeah, I'll stay with the wildcat. It'd be my pleasure." Donnie grins salaciously. Tess bares her teeth at him.

I ask her, "You'll be here when I get back?"

"Depends on how long you take mami, I'm going to work later, it's ladies' night."

After telling Dean to give me a minute to dress properly, I scurry to my room. In there, I exchanged my sweats for a pair of gym shorts and put on a bra for the first time today. Eyeing my sleep shirt for all of two seconds, I throw it on. Maybe I'm fooling myself into thinking it'll bring me comfort. Taking a deep dive into my demons isn't going to be easy. After pulling a sweater over the top, I slip on a pair of tennis shoes and leave the solace of my room. A heated debate over the best way to make a BLT sounds from the kitchen.

I can tell Donnie and Tess are going to get along fabulously.

Glancing at my watch, I realize it's already 2pm, we need to get going. As I pass Jeri's room, a shadow moves from inside. Tiptoeing closer, I peer in and catch a glimpse of Dean standing in the middle of her space, a unicorn stuffie in his hands. Leaning on the door frame, I observe him. There are trophies and medals stacked on a shelf above her desk, colored pencils in a cup, and half drawn sketches littering the surface. He runs his fingers over one, reverently, if I'm not mistaken it's a picture of a bird. What kind? I couldn't say. Jeri's got a vivid imagination. He eyes the shelf, and he reads each of the trophies on display.

"She likes soccer?" Startled, I jumped at the sound of his voice, I didn't realize he knew I was here.

Pushing past the tightness in my throat, "Oh, um, yes. She does." I laugh softly, "She's been a kicker since she discovered her feet, and I swear she was running before she was walking." Moving into the room with him, I picked up a medal and ran my thumb across the top, "When she was four, I put her in the youth league. It was something, watching them toddling around, they kicked each other more than the ball. Most of those are just participation trophies, but she insisted on putting them up. When we moved from our apartment, she packed them with her bedding. I haven't even gotten the rest of our things out of storage," I pause, "that's where you and I are going by the way."

He turns to me, brow raised sardonically "You're taking me to help you move the rest of your stuff?"

"Very funny." I dead pan.

He shrugs.

"No, I'm not taking you to help me move," I set the medal down and wring my hands together, "I'm taking you to see something."

Without another word I turn and walk away. Following me to the driveway, I clear my throat when he passes the truck and walks towards his bike. I'm not in any kind of emotional state to be glued to Dean's back. That wouldn't end well for either of us.

He clarifies, "I'm just moving it so we can get out."

Oh.

Ohhh.

Well now I feel stupid for assuming he'd want me pressed up against him. It does sound mighty fine too. Cataloging every dip and valley between the muscles. I'd love nothing more than to map it with my tongue.

The rumble of his straight pipes breaks me out of my fantasy, I scramble for the driver's side of my truck and after a few moments, he climbs in the cab with me.

We're silent during the entire hour-long drive to the storage units. We've moved so many times since Jericho's birth, I couldn't risk losing anything, so I took out this climate-controlled unit a couple of years ago. No one knows I have it, not even Thorne. Tessa leased it in her name and all my important things are safe if we need to leave in a hurry. All our photographs and papers are housed inside. When I pulled alongside the building, I put the truck in park but made no move to get out. At my hesitation, Dean turns, giving me his undivided attention.

His phone's been steadily going off the whole way here, but he's ignored it. Currently, it's buzzing like crazy in his pocket. "Are you going to answer that? If you've got business to take care of, I'd rather you do it now. Before we go down this rabbit hole."

Pulling it from his pocket, he silences it. "If it's important, Don can handle it for a while." he looks up at the building, "I thought we were going to get your daughter."

Gripping the steering wheel tight, I explain. "We're not going to get her just yet... we can't. Can you get eyes on her in the meantime if I give you the location of the camp?"

Nodding, although confused, he pulls his phone back out. I give him her location and wait as he sends a few text messages. When he's done, he tucks it away once more. "Saints Prez is familiar with the area. One of the brothers has a kid there, so we've already got people watching. She'll be safe for a bit and then we'll go get her."

Alright this is it.

Unable to look at him while I do this next part, I face the windshield. "Before we go in. I need to tell you a story." I pause, "I need to tell you about the days leading up to before I...." clearing my throat, "*you know*." when he still doesn't say anything, I keep going. "I need you to stay quiet and let me finish. Then, if you're up for it, we'll go in and I'll show you some things." I waited anxiously for him to respond.

Murmuring quietly, he gives me the go ahead.

"Tell me your story Songbird."

CHAPTER TWELVE

Sage, Age 18
FIVE DAYS BEFORE HER "DEATH"

Sneaking back in the house didn't go quite as well as sneaking out did. When I climbed onto my balcony, Hattie was sitting on my bed, wearing a miserable expression.

Well... fuck.

My 18th birthday was four days ago, but Hattie's kept me busy since. I've scrubbed, swept and mopped every inch of this house. She has 'company coming' is what she told me by way of explanation. Dean's father sent him on a run that took longer than planned, so we weren't able to spend time together in celebration until tonight. It's all we had since he's leaving first thing for another run.

Aunt Hat's been surprisingly sober the last week but acting more unstable by the day. When I suggested she take the edge off earlier, she relented, taking a deep dive into the bottle. That my friends, is how she was out for the count by 8:30, so I did what anyone else would do in my shoes... I left.

These past two years have been miserable, Fern went to live with her grandmother in Texas, Hattie wouldn't elaborate on why, one day she was here, the next she wasn't. We still talk when we can. I miss her like crazy. Then Thorne went off to the Air Force. Last I heard, the FBI recruited him into their training program. He'd mentioned coming to visit for my birthday, but I haven't seen him, not yet. My big brother doesn't break his promises, so I've been patient. It's been a nightmare though, I've been left here, alone, with her. Day in and day out. Suppose it could be worse. She hasn't physically touched me since I was 16, but words hurt just as badly. The threat of violence still hangs over my head, but I'm done walking on eggshells.

I've been counting down the days. Deans tried to get me to leave before now, but I don't want to risk him getting in trouble with the law. Hattie would call the cops in a hurry if she knew I was running away with him. Her disapproval has never been a secret, I've been called a 'biker's whore' so many times over the years. The insult has lost its effect. Now that I'm legally an adult, it'll happen, I'll finally be free. We've been waiting for the opportune time; Dean's dad has kept him so busy, poor Angus has thrown himself into club business ever since his wife died. After tonight, I won't see Dean for ten days, on his return, I'll leave this place with him for good.

We don't talk about what he does for the club. I know most of it is above board -at least I hope- but I'm aware they do some unsavory things. Truthfully, I just don't care. I know who Dean is, that's all that matters. I'll chase the darkness away for him.

I walk past Hattie, and she slurs, "Where the hell have you been?"

Pulling a fresh set of pajamas out of my drawer, I don't engage, not when she's like this. It won't do me any good and besides, it's none of her business. She staggers off my bed and follows me across the hall to the bathroom. When I try to close the door, she doesn't let me. It's awkward. Doing my best to ignore her presence, I turn on the shower and wait for it to warm up. Seems she's not leaving until I address her. Smothering my frustration, I ask, "What do you want Hat?"

Her face twists with rage, spittle at the corners of her lips. "I want what I'm owed and you're not going to ruin this for me by acting like a biker's whore."

Ahh, yes. This again.

When I just stare at her blankly, refusing to give her the reaction from me she so desperately craves; she storms out of the bathroom.

Shutting the door confused as ever, I mull it over. I have no idea what she's talking about, and I really don't care. In a few days, I'll never have to see her again. Testing the water, I step into the shower. This isn't the first time she's spouted nonsense, it won't be the last. As the spray crashes over me, I chalk it up to more drunken babbling and recall my night with Dean.

My Raven took me on a ride. My arms were wrapped tightly around his waist as I snuggled into his back. Bringing a hand back and gripping my thigh, he left it there for the entire ride while making soothing strokes. Once we finally stopped, I was so keyed up it wasn't funny. We'd barely climbed off his bike when I jumped in his arms, wrapping my legs around him like a koala. He laughed heartily before kissing me deeply, hands under my thighs, holding me to him. Without breaking the kiss, he walked me to the picnic he'd set up earlier in the evening.

It was perfect, he brought hot cocoa in a thermos and little ham sandwiches, nothing fancy but I loved it all the same. After assuring him I'd gotten my fill, he pulled a blanket from below his bike's seat and leaned back against an old oak tree. Sitting between his spread legs, I put my back to his chest, we sat in comfortable silence for a while as he twirled a stray curl around his finger. Hugging me to him, he whispers, "I have a house for us."

Twisting in his hold, I take in his face. He's serious. I assumed we'd maybe stay at the clubhouse; this is so much better. The smile on his face is blinding and I find myself smiling back, "Really?"

Leaning in, he kisses me softly and pulls a key from his pocket. "I was waiting to surprise you, but I need you to know, I couldn't wait. I'm going on this run for Pop's and then I'm taking a break for a while. He's agreed to let me work in the garage and only send me out when he really needs me, one of his old timers can step in as VP," he pauses, leaning in again, brushing his lips against mine, "I want to start a life with you Songbird."

"What would that look like?" I whisper back.

Closing his eyes, as if picturing it, he answers me. "Waking up beside you every day, going to bed with you at night. Taking you out on dates. No more sneaking around, no more leaving you when I don't want to. We'd be together, in every way that matters. I'll marry you when you're ready, build a family. It'd be you and me Songbird."

I can't take it anymore. My heart is a war drum in my chest. Curling my arms around his neck, I position myself so I'm straddling his lap. While running my fingers through his hair, I tilt his face where I want it. I whisper back, "Yes."

My mouth slams down over his and I swallow his groan. His hands encompass my waist, and I slowly roll my hips into his hardness. This isn't enough, I need skin on skin.

"More." I whisper.

Pulling back, I grip my sweater and pull it over my head before making quick work of his. After the fabric is gone, he trails his tongue along the pillow of my breast, following a path upward. Moving my curtain of hair to the side, he places bites at the curve of my neck, dragging his teeth along my shoulder. Reaching back, I unhook my bra; the straps puddle loosely on my arms, impatiently, Dean groans and drags it the rest of the way, tossing it somewhere behind us. I'm shivering, but it's not from the cold.

"I need you Songbird."

Bringing his hands back up, he palms me, gently rolling my nipples between his fingers, I arch further into his hold. With his hands on me, I reach between us and unbutton his jeans. Shifting his hips so I can tug them down slightly, then I'm pulling him out. Stroking up and down, loving the velvety feel of him. He leans forward, taking a nipple into his mouth, biting gently on the puckered bud and I mewl.

Without warning, he stands, pulling my leggings and underwear down in one fell swoop. Grabbing the blanket, he throws it around my shoulders before scooping me up, my legs instinctively wrapped around his waist, like two puzzle pieces. When my back hits the tree, the blanket protecting my skin, Dean peppers me with more kisses, his length nudging against my inner thigh.

He adjusts so he's holding me with one arm, slipping the other hand between my folds, "You're so wet for me Songbird." he groans, two fingers push inside me, as he rubs my clit with his thumb and adds pressure, I cry out. "You going to be good and come for me?"

All I can do is nod.

Finding that sweet spot inside, he starts rubbing it slowly. After a few passes, he uses his thighs to hold my weight and bring his other hand down. When he pinches my clit, that's what sends me over the edge, pure ecstasy sweeps me away. Before I have a chance to come down from my orgasm, he picks me back up higher and inches inside me. It's slow at first, he's holding back.

I slowly roll my hips in sync with his, causing us both to moan as he slides into the hilt. Restraint snapping, he unravels, moving with intensity. With the pace increasing, I cry out. He pistons his hips, hands gripping so tight I'll have bruises. Tugging his mouth to mine, our tongues tangle in harmony when suddenly he rips away and commands in a rasping growl, "Come for me Songbird."

I do, I totally fucking do.

There's a tingling heat inside me as his movements get jerky, after a few more pumps I can feel every bit of him finishing. When I've come down from my high, Dean is panting. Both arms banded around my waist. I plant sweet kisses on his forehead, his cheeks, then his lips. He lowers me to my feet and tightens the blanket around me more securely. Concern lining his brow, "Shit, I'm sorry Sage. I didn't think... I didn't use a condom."

Oh no. I didn't think either.

I look around, trying to find my clothes, reassuring him as I move. "It's okay. I'll run and get a plan B tomorrow."

Lifting my face, he kisses me gently and mutters another sorry. I wave away his worries. "It'll be okay. It was only one time."

When I step out of the shower, I take my time getting dressed. My neck has a few love bites, but I feel no shame. When I make it back to my room, I shut and lock my door before snuggling under the blankets. With our future on my mind, I quickly fell asleep.

CHAPTER THIRTEEN
FOUR DAYS BEFORE HER "DEATH"

I wake up to a morning text. Missing him already.

Raven: 10 days baby. Then you're all mine. I love you Songbird.

Smiling to myself, I send one back.

Songbird: I can't wait. Love you too Raven.

After dressing, I make my way downstairs. The house is quiet. I'm assuming Aunt Hat is still sleeping off her bender, but I'd be wrong. When I step into the kitchen, she's standing at sink. Staring out of the window above, sipping coffee. Without turning, she says, "There's more in the pot."

Strange. But okay. I make my way over and fix up a cup the way I like and pop two pieces of bread into the toaster. When I'm pulling a jar of jam from the pantry, she says, "We need to talk this morning." There's no venom or vitriol in her voice. She sounds tired. Once I've finished slathering a heaping amount of jam on my toast, I join her at the breakfast table. Chewing slowly, I take notice of a few things. The bags under her eyes are more pronounced today and they're more bloodshot than usual. Did she not get any sleep? Is she still drunk from yesterday? If I didn't know any better, I'd say she's been crying. But Hattie Mason would have to be an actual human being for that.

Before I have a chance to read too much into it, she starts succinctly. "You're planning to leave, aren't you? With Dean, the biker boy?"

Ignoring the dig, I nod once while answering honestly. "I am."

Hattie plays with a chip on her mug then glances towards the window once more, "There's something you should know."

Setting my toast back on my plate, I'm giving her my undivided attention. "Okay. What do I need to know?"

She brings her coffee to her lips, taking a heavy drink before setting it back down delicately. Those bright blue eyes meet mine before her lips tug up slightly, then she completely floors me.

"There are men around the grounds with instructions to keep you here."

Wiggling a finger in each of my ears, I'm trying to make sure there's nothing obstructing my hearing. Positive that's not what she just said. At my clear unacceptance to her claim, the slight tug to her lips grows into a serpent's smile.

"You heard me." she nods, "There are men all around the grounds. They'll be here until the boss shows up to collect you himself."

I laugh, assuming she's drunk. Or high maybe? "I'm sorry, but the who is coming to get me?"

She's still smiling wickedly, "The Pakhan, the leader of the Medvedev Bratva. In a few days, he's coming to get what's due to him and coming to give me what's owed to me after all these years."

"I'm sorry, but are you out of your mind?"

Arching a brow in triumph, she gestures for me to look outside for myself.

Scooting my chair back quickly, I surged towards the window she was just staring out of. Sure enough, there are men at the barn, I glance to my right and see one close to the front porch. Hattie's chair scrapes before I feel her presence as she saddles up beside me. The look on her face is the happiest I've seen it. When I turn to leave, she grabs my arm roughly. Dragging me to the table, she flings me back into my vacated seat.

"You will sit. You will listen, or I'll call the men in here. Trust when I say, they will do far worse to you than me." finger pointed in my face; eyes wild. I know she means it. She wouldn't hesitate to call them in.

Satisfied I've gotten the message, she settles back in her own seat slowly. Once upon a time, Hattie was a beautiful woman. Her ice blue eyes, and white-blonde hair are still pretty, but the venom she spews, and the excessive drinking haven't done her any favors.

Disassociating for a moment, I fixate on the ruddiness in her cheeks and nose when I snap out of it, remembering what she said, "Why is someone coming to collect me?"

She scoffs, like it's the most obvious answer to a stupid question, "Because you were always his."

I snarl back, "I think the fuck not. Are you insane? I want nothing to do with whatever this is."

Hattie laughs at that, so hard tears trek down her cheeks. When she composes herself and wipes the tears away, she levels me with a disbelieving gaze. "Oh, you naive little girl." Shaking her head, "You've never had the right to choose. You were born and that choice was stripped. No women in that world get a say, nothing more than high dollar chattel, bartered with because they have the right bloodline."

She's serious.

"What does my bloodline have to do with this?"

Sighing, she looks at the photographs on the wall before answering vaguely, "Everything."

I'm getting frustrated, "You can't keep me locked here. I'm a person. I have rights. If Dean gets back and I'm gone, he will look for me. He will follow."

Cutting her eyes at me she murmurs, "Then he'd be even more foolish than I thought. The Pakhan wasn't happy when he learned you've been whoring yourself out to a low life biker. I convinced him you needed to have your fun, ultimately, he understood that. You're young. It was generous of him to allow you the dalliance, but now the time has come for it to end. Dean was never going to be a permanent thing." She brings both hands to the table and claps them together, leaning in, "He also wasn't happy to learn you intended to run away, you stupid girl. Thus, the predicament we're in now. He'd be here himself, but he has matters to attend to. Sending his men ahead to keep you in place was the solution."

Tears are tracking down my face, I swipe my cheeks angrily. "I'm 18. I don't have to stay here."

She nods, "You're right. You don't. Good luck going anywhere though. We're both trapped here for the time being. I'm going to give it to you straight Sage, you need to understand what's coming, consider it a mercy."

When I don't interrupt, she keeps going. I'm shaking with rage.

"You have been promised the leader of the Medvedev Bratva since you were four years old, that's the Russian mafia, in case you were unaware. My husband Clay was in deep with them. He was what you would consider a 'cleaner', if they needed a body disposed of, he took care of it. They utilized his skills often. The man may have been an idiot, but he was very good at what he did. Thorough, efficient. His greatest downfall was the gambling problem he never addressed."

Walking across the kitchen, she brings back a bottle of whiskey. Pouring a heavy dose into her coffee and taking a sip before continuing. "Clay owed a lot of money to a lot of people around the time your parents died. The agreement with the last Pakhan was for us to take you in and he'd wipe Clay's debt. We had to move from the city I loved to this shit hole my parents left me. But that's beside the point. As I was saying, Clay, the idiot, got himself killed by the Irish Mob when he was on a job, didn't realize someone was waiting for him to show. It was a set up. They tortured him for days until he gave them what he knew. Clay was responsible for revealing Vasily's location, hammering the final nail in that particular coffin - that's the last leader of the Bratva if you're still following me, the last Pakhan- anyhow, you were already in my care at the time. A few days later, I was informed nothing would change. There was still a need for you to be hidden and cared for. I'd receive a monthly stipend and an added bonus once you were of age. So that's what I've done. Understand? You're a chess piece on a large board. It's time to move you. You. Owe. Me."

I'm trying to wrap my head around all the information she's just dropped on me. There are still so many things I don't understand, but like a dumbass, I ask a question I already know the answer to, "You're not really my aunt, are you?"

She laughs boisterously, "Oh God no." waving me away as if it's the funniest thing she's ever heard.

"Did Thorne or Fern know?"

A look of something akin to guilt crosses her face, "No. They knew what I told them. You were a cousin; they chose to treat you like a sibling. But Fern, I couldn't have that, couldn't have her involved with you. She's so young. So good. Her grandmother offered to take her, so I sent her away. Because. Of. You." She jabs a finger at me, spittle forming at the corners of her mouth as her temper starts to run away from her, "You planted ideas in my girl's head. She stopped trusting me, started asking too many questions. I didn't have a choice. You took my girl from me, you tried to take my boy from me too. He rarely comes home now."

Backing up in my chair, I held up my hands in defense, "I did no such thing. You're a raging alcoholic Hat. The only person you to blame for things is yourself."

Slamming a hand on the table she screeches, "That's not true! If I'd never gotten saddled up with you my kids would still be here, if Clay hadn't agreed to take you in, he'd still be alive. He was an idiot, but he was my idiot! He had to take every job they told him to, with you here, it tied him in even more and he got killed for it!"

"That had absolutely nothing to do with me! I was a child. You just told me that Clay had a gambling problem, that's not on me. I'm sorry if you feel like it's my fault, but it isn't. You need to do some self-reflection Hattie Mason."

Pacing, she picks up the bottle, drinking straight from it. Every so often she's looking at me with venom. I'm trying to figure the best path out of the kitchen when she snarls at me. "You and your fucking family were the end of us."

"Who are my parents then?" I ask through gritted teeth.

Her eyes take on a hard edge, "There's a gag order in place, even now I'm not supposed to say. The most important thing you can take from this is you'll be the bridge to end the war and get the Pakhan what he wants. He's going to marry you, breed you and if you're lucky, he'll keep you."

"I will not marry him. He can't force me."

Like night and day, her bipolar shows. She blinks rapidly at me, then laughs condescendingly. "I assure you, he can. He's been waiting for the day he can pull one over on the McGregor Clan, you're the ticket. I suggest you go to your room for a bit. Let all this sink in. Get out of my sight before I do something I regret."

she waves me away in dismissal before calling out, "Don't bother trying to contact Dean, they've got something scrambling the cells. You'll be gone in a few days."

The McGregor Clan? Who the fuck are they?

Once upstairs, I'm pacing like an animal at the zoo. So much information to process, but unfortunately, she's right. I tried to call Dean immediately after locking myself in my room, but no calls would go out and my texts show 'undeliverable'. First things first, I won't stay here, locked up. If I can get out, if I can make it to the clubhouse, I know the brothers there will protect me. Angus will protect me. Donnie should still be in town, he's who usually looks after me when Dean's gone.

I need a plan.

From my second story balcony, I can see each man clearly. They seem to be rotating around the perimeter. Charging back to my desk, I grab a notepad and tally how many men there are and then write their descriptions down. 'Tall guy', 'bald guy', 'short guy', 'red shirt dude', going on and on until I think I've gotten them all. The rest of the afternoon is spent counting the minutes between rotations and learning their pattern. It's a test of my patience, having to wait for nightfall to make my move. Dean's voice echoes in my head, encouraging me, *'you can do this Songbird'*.

Around dinner time, I tiptoe downstairs. Food wasn't a priority today, but if I'm going to be running like my life depends on it, I'll need the fuel.

Luckily, the kitchen is empty, and I eat in relative peace before making my way back upstairs. Hurrying to my closet, I dump the contents of my backpack before throwing in a few changes of clothes, making sure to grab Dean's football shirt. That will always go with me. I slip into my trainers and pull my hair into a tight braid. The hoodie I've got is one of Dean's, luckily my man favors black, I need to blend into the night as well as he would.

Pacing only increases my anxiety, forcing myself to stop, I rest and watch the men move around.

It seems dark enough.

Checking my phone again, I see I've got about ten minutes until the next rotation, then 45 seconds to shimmy down the lattice and make a break for the tree line. Slipping my pack on my shoulders and tucking my braid into the hood of my shirt, I lock my bedroom door and wait.

'Now. Go now Songbird.'

On soft feet, I go through the balcony doors and pull them shut behind me. Flinging my leg over the banister, I slide my foot to the first lattice rung and carefully maneuver onto it. This old thing has held up over the years, please don't let tonight be the night it doesn't. I send up a silent prayer to whoever is listening and drop my full weight on it. It creaks quietly but holds. I make quick work of the descent, once my feet hit soft grass, I stay low and tie the straps of my backpack around my waist before moving. I don't need the jostle of it giving me away. Once I start running, I'm not fucking stopping. When I pop up, there doesn't appear to be anyone around. In fast strides, I hightail it towards my willow. If I can just get far enough out to send a message, someone will be able to help me finish my escape.

I'm controlling my breathing, thanking God for all those years of cross country, when I hear the first shout behind me. Someone starts yelling, then multiple shouts reach me, seems like the alarms been sounded.

I'm not fucking stopping. I can't.

My legs are pumping so hard I'm flying. In a dead sprint, I'm almost to the willow, if I can get under the coverage, I can flee into the tree line. From there it's about five miles to the clubhouse. That's nothing for me. Footsteps thunder in the distance and the engine of a vehicle fires up.

Six feet left.

Adrenaline surging, I put on more speed and break through the willow wisps full charge.

I've just gotten to my haven when I hit what feels like a brick wall. Slamming me with such intensity I close line. My back collides with the ground, and my knees hit my chest, knocking the wind from my sails. As I lay gasping, a man laughs. "Stupid bitch.

Hattie saunters up beside him, looking down at me with a smirk. "I told you she'd try to run."

That fucking bitch. Miserable fucking cunt.

I can't speak yet, but if I could. I'd call her every name I could think of. Hattie positions herself directly over me and glances up at the man with a nod. He rears back and the last thing I see before his fist meets my face, is the sadistic smile on hers.

Then nothing but black.

CHAPTER FOURTEEN
THE DAY BEFORE SHE "DIED"

I've been in the abandoned barn for what feels like an eternity. My arms are numb from the way I'm trussed up in one of the stalls, a rope is tied around my wrists and I'm strung up from the top of the empty stall, hanging here like a sack of shit. My face hurts like a sonofabitch, one eye is swollen shut and I'm fairly sure my ribs are cracked. 'Bald guy' walks into the barn to check on me. Through streams of sunlight, I try and fail to keep the smug smile off my face. I didn't go without a fight. When I woke as they were pulling me towards the barn, I fought like hell. The swelling under 'bald guys' eyes has me immensely proud of myself. One swift kick while he was wrangling me, and I broke his fat nose.

If I could have stopped there I would have, instead I continued to pop off. Not my finest moment but losing my temper and calling him a 'pussy' probably wasn't the smartest thing in the world. The split in my lip is a fun little reminder to shut up.

Consequences they said. The longer I sway here, hopelessness trickles into my being. It's getting harder to hold my head up, each breath is weighted and I'm so very tired.

Soft footsteps perk my ears, not one of the men. When Hattie pushes open the stall door, I train my one good eye on her, tracking her every move. She sets a bottle of water down on the straw covered floor.

"It didn't have to be like this you know?" She scolds, "If you'd have just stayed in your room like a good girl, Viktor wouldn't have laid a hand on you. I told you they were here under instructions not to let you leave. Instead, you take off and *hurt yourself.*"

My mouth is dry as the Sahara, but I manage to croak out incredulously. "Hurt myself?"

Sighing, she ignores my question, like this is one big inconvenience for her. "I've brought you some water." grabbing the bottle she holds it to my mouth, "Drink girl."

She grips my chin roughly, tilting my head so she can pour it in my mouth. I'm drowning. More water spills down my face than I can swallow, my throat is too dry. Pushing my discomfort deep I try to take what I can get. Just that little bit has already helped my delirium. When she lets me go, she dusts her hands off on the back of her jeans. The fog clearing from my head, I notice she looks more put together today. I can still smell the slight traces of whiskey on her, but it looks like she made an actual effort with her appearance.

"How long have I been in here?" My voice is a whisper.

"A few days. Not to worry, my company will be here tomorrow night sometime. He'll get you sorted when he collects you. He's been apprised of the fact you tried to run and that you injured yourself during the process. There's a doctor on standby for situations such as these. You should really be more careful the next time you go running in the dark Sage."

That does it, I laugh. And I laugh, and I laugh. I'm laughing so hard that it hurts everywhere, but I can't stop. It's demented. I have no control over it. Tears streak down my face and the laughter is intermingled with sobs. But still, I laugh.

Raising her voice over my clear nervous breakdown, Hattie informs me that Thorne is here for a visit. She's broken the news of my upcoming departure to him, claiming he thought it was 'probably the best thing for me'.

Betrayal settles deep in my gut. With the realization that my brother -*no, not my brother*-, would leave me to this fate. My laughter dies slowly, but the sobs increase in intensity. Great heaving cries rock my body. Her news finally cracked the dam I tried to keep glued together. No one's coming for me.

Eventually, the man with the broken nose must tire of my cries, I look him in the eye, practically begging for him to put me out of my misery. Thankfully, he does. With a sadistic grin, his arm rears back, then it's lights out all over again.

CHAPTER FIFTEEN
THE MORNING SHE "DIED"

Sometime later -an hour, a day, a year maybe- my name harshly whispered pulls me from a dreamless sleep. There's a jerk at my wrists before a warm body brushes up against mine. It's dark, too dark to see anything clearly. When my wrists are free from their bindings, my body falls like a downed tree. The dirt covered floor rustles and then I'm being lifted by strong arms.

"Shhh, I know it hurts. But you've got to be quiet, we don't have much time." My head lolls to the side when I recognize Thorne's voice. He props me against the barn wall and shines a light in my eyes. It's too much after the shadowed stall, I flinch. Gently, he pulls my swollen lid open, I assume to see if I'm concussed.

I could have told him I most definitely am.

My brother mutters a quiet 'fuck' into the room. "You're right, you've got a concussion and definite dehydration."

How long is too long?

"It's been three days."

Did I ask that out loud?

"You did."

Oh. Fuck. I did it again.

I gasp when he starts rubbing down my arms, assessing the other damage, "What are you doing?"

Each nerve is tingling, lightening shooting through my limbs. Finally lifting my head to see him, he looks at me like I'm crazy. "I thought it was obvious. I'm breaking you out."

I narrow one eye with suspicion. I might've narrowed both, but ya know, only one is functional. "So you say, I thought this was the best thing for me?"

Head rearing back in shock, he questions, "Why would I ever be okay with this? You're my sister no matter what. When I found out what was going on." he swallows audibly, "And who you really are. No way in hell was I going to stand by. I pretended with my mother, but never with you. Trust me, I have a plan."

I'm not in a position to look a gift horse in the mouth, I'm tired. So very tired. Thorne seems sincere enough; he's never given me a reason to doubt him before. It's Hattie's word against his, and let's be honest, Hattie's a fucking liar. Taking a gamble, I nodded my head, relenting.

"Call Dean." I plead.

He looks conflicted as he crouches in front of me. "I can't."

When I start to protest, he gently takes my hand in his, "I don't think it's safe for him to know about this. He'll do something reckless and end up getting himself killed. You don't understand what's happening." his voice takes on a serious edge, "The Ravens MC is allied with the Irish Mob Sage. Angus sends his men on runs for them... sometimes hits. This conflict has been going on for years and at this moment, tensions are extremely high." he pauses to wipe my face with his shirt, when I don't react, he keeps going, "You know who I work for? Well, they like the status quo as it is. If Medvedev gets you, this war will turn into something nuclear. McGregor would risk it all, burn everything to the ground. Two days ago, I walked through the door to see you, only to learn about this. Mom told me everything. I played along but used my sat phone to contact a friend at the agency."

My heart is a drum beat in my chest. I don't think I can take much more. Emotions are flooding through me too quickly to name. Fear being the most prominent.

"I'm going to hide you. No one can know. If Colin knew you were alive out there, it would fuck with the bureau's plans. I know it isn't right or fair. But you've got to understand, Colin McGregor is not a rational man when it comes to family. He's been mourning you for years. You are the tide that will turn the war one way or another. My instructions were clear. The bureau is keeping this off the record. Only a handful of trusted agents will know the truth. It's not permanent. Dean can't know because he'll do something stupid, and you'll be compromised. His feelings for you will only get him killed. The guy is my best friend, but I know him. You do too. He'd never let you go willingly and if he goes with you, he'd be leaving everything behind, you don't want that on your conscious. Not to mention, I'm not entirely sure McGregor will be thrilled to learn about your relationship. This will keep you safe from Medvedev too. Sage, I need you to trust me."

My one good eye darts back and forth between his, none of this is making any sense, "But Dean and I are supposed to start a life together. If you called him... if he knew...."

He interrupts me before I can finish, "Sage, no. This is your life I'm talking about. If Dean knows, you'd be putting yourself in danger. We can't tell him."

I still don't fully understand, but I don't want Dean in danger because of me. I'm scared.

"Who am I to McGregor?" the question is whispered; I almost think he's not going to answer me. With the shake of his head and a pleading apology in his gaze, he does.

"Probably the most important person in his life. You're his daughter, the heir everyone assumed died."

I finally have a name for what I'm feeling. Pure. Heartbreak. It's physical, I'm being torn in half. I don't want to leave Dean; I don't want him dead even more. Thorne could be right; Dean's protective nature would prevail. He'd lose his mind and his life in the process. Maybe this is better? Maybe me leaving would be easier on him. This is all too much. Taking just a moment, I try to compartmentalize everything he's just shared. Thorne's never given me a reason to distrust him and we're running out of time, any minute the guards will come back. With only one choice to make. I lean over, vomiting nothing. Dry heaves rack my body and my brother leans in, holding me steady. From my position on the floor, I look up and rasp out, "What's your plan?"

He grins sadly, "I'm going to burn the barn down."

CHAPTER SIXTEEN
Dean

The silence was loud when Sage finished telling her story. She never made eye contact with me, not once. I listened intently as her voice shook and her lips quivered. The fear was real, and when she got to the part where she'd made the decision to leave? Anguish lined her face, as tears flowed in steady rivulets. Truthfully, I don't know how I feel, and I'm not sure my feelings matter, not in comparison to that. Not when she went through so much. So many fucked up things, and I was there for none of it.

No, I was gone. I never should have left her.

She survived something horrendous.

Even damning me, she saved me in the process.

I'm not sure how to reconcile the two.

Thorne showing up when he did was a miracle, but fuck.

Only God knows what would have happened had he decided to

visit home a week later. Would I have put myself at risk? Yes. A thousand times over if it meant keeping Sage safe. But putting *her* at risk? Not in a million years. Thorne was wrong about that. If they'd called me, I would have left everything behind. I would have gone anywhere, done anything.

All this time wasted.

So many things make sense now. Why the Russians are here, why Thorne went through great lengths to hide her. Why they faked her death. And McGregor? Her father? Fuck me. If the man knew about this, he'd annihilate everyone involved.

Does it mean I'm okay with being kept in the dark? No.

Do I understand it? Kind of.

Sage breaks her stare off with the windshield, turning to face me. I've yet to utter a word, really, what could I even say? I wouldn't even know where to begin, or how to convey the multitude of things I'm feeling. Starting with something simple sounds safe enough.

Clearing my throat, I ask, "What happened after he burned the barn down?"

"I was in and out of consciousness for a while. When I finally came to, I was somewhere I'd never been before. Leather sofas and finished concrete flooring. I was all alone." she hesitates, "But when I started exploring, I realized I was standing in what would have been our home."

Unable to conceal my shock, my mouth gapes open as I process this. She was there and I didn't even know.

"You were in the house I bought for us? How long?"

"Just a day."

I didn't go home for five more days. Not a trace of her was left behind.

"Alright, Thorne took you to the house, then what?"

"I guess he went back to Hattie's, they were dealing with the aftermath of the barn burning. If he took off too soon, it would be suspicious. Someone was sent to get me, they moved me to Memphis for a while. After that, I moved to Georgia, then Florida. His friend at the bureau got me a new identity. Moving was the smart choice, but I finally got to a point where I couldn't keep uprooting. Jericho couldn't do it anymore. She needed stability. I met Tessa when I was in Florida. Together, we picked New Orleans. That girl has her own demons she's running from, so we decided to do it together."

Rubbing my hands along my jeans, I try to imagine myself in her shoes. Leaving everything you know, hiding. Surviving. While towing along a child? This woman was strong, and she deserved to know.

"You are a warrior, Sage." I whispered reverently.

The tears that had slowed started flowing faster, her bottom lip pulled between her teeth. She scrunched her eyes tightly and brought her thumb and forefinger to the bridge of her nose. Swallowing hard, she breathed in through her nose and out through her lips. With somewhat more composure, she brought her eyes back, meeting mine.

"There's more."

I gestured to her to continue. So far gone from words.

Reaching for the truck door, she opened it and climbed out. Field trip time? When we walked to the storage building door, she typed in a code, and it unlocked. She held the door for me as we walked through, the mechanisms whirred, and it locked back automatically. The corridors were long, shiny white tile clacked under our feet. For a storage unit, this one was nice. Rental fees had to be a pretty penny. She made a right turn and then a left. Midway down she stopped in front of a small garage door. Squatting down, she produced a small key from her pocket and undid the padlock. Once the door was raised, she paused at the threshold.

Under lowered lashes, she whispered, "Forgive me."

I'm working on it, truly. I'm trying to understand, if I could explain how I felt, I would. The human mind is a complex thing. For the most part, I'm good at putting my feelings in boxes and then cataloging those boxes onto shelves. They collect in a dusty room hidden in the back of my mind. But this? The box won't close. Every time I try, the lid just blows open.

With nothing else to say, I ask, "Are we going in?"

With a sharp nod, she marched on. I leaned off to the side and watched as she rifled through plastic storage bins. After pulling one from the very back, she approached me gingerly and set it gently on top of a stack next to where I was standing.

"Open it."

With shaking hands, I did just that.

There were pictures inside, hundreds of them. Sage smiling with Tessa in front of the bar. Sage pregnant, hands resting on her swollen stomach. Sage and Tessa sightseeing. Sage laying in a hospital bed with a bundled baby on her chest.

Where is the father?

Shuffling through the pictures, I was getting small glimpses of her life. Setting that stack down, I looked at her before picking up the next. There was something I was missing. She'd started pacing, thumbnail pressed between her lips as she chewed it. Catching me staring, she stopped abruptly and looked at the stack in my hand. Bright eyes met mine and she grimaced, an apology written on her face. Curious, I finally looked down.

A little girl smiled back at me with a dimpled grin and two missing teeth. She had black curls and silver eyes, with a smattering of freckles across her nose and cheeks matching her mother's. She couldn't have been more than five years old here. My breath whooshed out of me at once. Clutching the photo tighter, I looked at Sage in disbelief.

"This is your daughter?" I choked out.

"Not just mine, *ours*."

My knees buckled, hitting the concrete floor before I could stop it. Sage surged towards me, but I held up a hand, halting her. If she touched me right now, I don't know what I'd do. It was taking everything in me to keep it together. I prided myself on the control I've learned over the last eight years. My walls were breaking, and I was slipping. The maelstrom of emotions was like an earthquake, threatening to undo everything, if she touched me, I'd lose it all. Every brick would tumble. We didn't have time for that.

"I need a minute." I gritted out through clenched teeth.

She nodded her head in understanding and backed away. "If you hate me now, I'd understand."

There was nothing I trusted myself to say. I didn't hate her, the opposite in fact, I would always love her. No matter what she did or would do. She'd always be mine, but this, this *hurts*. I have a daughter out in the world I've never met, I've missed everything. Betrayals have sliced me left and right in the last 48 hours. Time, just a bit, was all I needed to figure out the best path forward.

First, I needed to call my brother.

Rising from my knees, I ran my thumb over the photo before pocketing it. Striding past her, I ignore her devastated face and follow the exits signs. Stepping out into the sunshine, I pull my phone from my pocket and dial Donnie. He answered after only a few rings.

"You good D?"

Laughing manically, because I was the farthest thing from good, I answered. "Peachy."

"Very convincing."

"I will be."

"That works for me. I'm with you, brother. You know this."

I knew he was. Don's been the one constant in my life. Never faltering.

"The little girl is mine Don."

A pause before he curses under his breath, "You're serious?"

Pulling the photo from my pocket, I snapped a picture of it and sent it to my brother. Waiting for him to see.

"She looks just like you Aberdean." his voice is soft, awed.

"I know."

"What are we going to do from here? She's at camp, right? We go get her? I'm not comfortable with my niece being away while all this is going on."

That's all it took for him to accept her. My word and a photograph. She'll have his loyalty until the day he dies.

"That's the plan. Sage is going to head over and collect her when we're done here. Do me a solid and arrange for security to follow her. I need to meet with Petey, go over the latest information. There's so much more Don. We need to call church, update Jora, but knowing that fucker, he already knows."

I can practically hear his head nodding over the line, "Yeah do that. Tessa's already gone to work; I went with her. Want me to have a prospect come here too, keep an eye on her?"

"That sounds solid. Make sure whoever they send keeps a low profile, no cut. When they show, meet me at the Saints. I'm going to have Sage take me to my bike, I'll head over from there... also, I need to tell Dad."

There's a pause before he hangs up, "Dad may already be aware, if Jora knows, you know he told him too. Pop's may be waiting for you to call first. You know how he is. As for Sage, don't be too hard on her Dean. From what I could coax out of Tess, she's missed you." I disconnect without responding, ignoring his advice. Jora doesn't answer when I call, so I shoot off a text as I hear the door lock back into place behind me.

Sage walks towards the truck with another small container in her hands. Opening the back door, she places it gently on the seat before moving to the driver's side door and climbing in.

Muttering out a prayer for patience, I climb in too.

We're 15 minutes into the drive when she breaks the silence. "Do you have any questions? I mean, I'm sure you do. That was dumb to ask. I'll tell you whatever you want to know."

There's only one thing that I need an answer to, what she says will decide how we move forward.

"Did you hide your pregnancy before you left?"

Head snapping in my direction, she turns the steering wheel with her, almost running us off the road. Reaching over, I grab the wheel and correct it. Mouth agape, she asks, "Why would I... no Dean. I didn't hide anything. Why would you even ask that?"

Truthfully, I need to lash out. The beast in my chest wants to hurt her, like she's hurt me. Shrugging with indifference I don't really feel, I murmur, "You hid everything else. What's one more thing?"

It's a jab, one she doesn't deserve, but my rationale isn't functioning. I understood her leaving, but this is big. I need to know that she didn't hide it from me before disappearing into the night.

Still staring in my direction, we start to veer off the road again. Realizing what she's doing, she adjusts the wheel before whipping us into an alcove hidden by trees. Driving about a half mile down the dirt path before she stops, throws the truck in park and jumps out, clearly rattled. I heave myself from my seat and follow, she doesn't go far before she starts pacing. She's 10ft from me when she turns -anger twisting her face into a malicious snarl- stomping over and jabs a finger in my chest.

"I had no idea I was pregnant until four months after I left! You remember the last time we were together? *You didn't use a condom Dean.* I told you not to worry, one time wouldn't hurt. I'd just grab a plan B." Clapping her hands together sarcastically she continues, "Tell me *asshole*, at which point in my story do you think I was able to do that? Hmm? By the time I'd left, I'd forgotten all about our little mishap, assuming I was sick from the stress. It was only when I passed out and was rushed to the ER did I find out I was 17 weeks pregnant Aberdean. I did the best I could considering our circumstances! I wanted to tell you so many times. *So. Many. Fucking. Times.* But when I knew of her existence, it wasn't just me anymore. I had to protect her. So, I did. We were supposed to do that together! Build a life together, remember? Do you think there's ever a moment when I look at her that I don't think of you? You've seen her Dean. That girl is your mirror!"

"You should have told me!" I bellow, pulling my hair at the roots, "At any point in time you could have called! We would have worked it out! Don't you understand that? I'd have done anything for you! *For our daughter!*"

Her face pinches before shaking her head in determination, "That wasn't a risk I was willing to take."

I snarl back, "It wasn't only your call! Not when you held life inside you, life that was half mine. Thorne was wrong. God damn it, Sage! Thorne. Was. Wrong. I would have left in a heartbeat. You were my entire world for years, fucking years Sage! I deserved to know. There was absolutely no reason for you to be alone all this time, no reason I shouldn't have been told the truth! And then I walk into a bar and see you? Are you serious? You and your fucking brother hid so many things! I was miserable Songbird. I've been miserable for years."

Stepping back as if I've slapped her, she sucks air into her lungs, "That's not fair Dean. I was between a rock and hard place, trying to do the best I could."

"The best you could? The best you... No Sage, you were listening to fucking Thorne. He was wrong. I don't know why he said all those things, but he was wrong."

Shaking her head, she looks at me sadly. I'm trembling, from rage, from sorrow, from adrenaline. A combination of all three.

"I'm sorry Dean. I don't know how many times I can say it. I've lived all these years in regret, but I can't change it, I knew I'd never earn redemption, knew I'd never earn your forgiveness. I didn't expect it. I just needed you to understand."

I slam a hand down on the hood of the truck and she jumps. Stepping away, I take several deep centering breaths, trying to calm myself. Bending at the waist, I run my hands through my hair and pull it back. Once I'm finished, I feel marginally calmer, but the anger is still there, the beast is pacing across his cage, scraping his nails against my ribs. While I do love her, at this moment I hate her too.

"I'm angry that you believed the lies you were fed, that you ate every word he said to get you out of that barn. I'm angry that you hid my daughter's existence from me for eight fucking years."

When she starts to cut back in, I hold a hand up, silencing her. "Let me finish. I'm angry and I'm entitled to be, but I understand Songbird. If it came down to me or you, I'd choose you every time. You should have chosen me too."

Snapping her mouth shut, her chest heaves. Sage looks so alive in this moment, face flush with indignation.

I want to kiss her.

Where the fuck that thought came from, no idea. But once I think it, it doesn't go away. The desire hits me with such intensity I have to physically hold myself back.

I want to ravage her.

Still, the thoughts keep pouring in as she puffs up again, readying herself to lay into me.

Fuck, I really, really want to kiss her.

Desperately.

Fuck it.

When she opens her mouth to argue some more, that's when I grab her by the nape and slam my lips over hers, stunned, she pulls back on a gasp and smacks me in the face. Her eyes glitter, like a lightning strike on the tumultuous sea. When I run my tongue over my stinging bottom lip, we stare at each other, her scowling, me baring my teeth. Both of us breathing unevenly.

Maybe this is what we need.

Faster than I can react, she's lunging forward, pushing me. I let her, "Take it out on me Songbird. Give it to me, all your hurt, all your rage. You were alone for so long, give me all your anger. Burn with me."

Blue eyes wild, pupils dilated, I can tell she's walking a fine line between rage and lust. She shoves me again, growling with frustration when I don't move. Digging in, she adds more force to her next assault. But I'm a brick wall. In anger, she shrieks and beats her fists on my chest in rapid succession, I barely feel it. Too focused on the way her lips felt on mine.

Finally, out of steam, she rears back huffing.

I'm expecting her to rage at me some more, but to my ever-loving shock, she throws her arms around my neck and pulls my mouth down to hers. It doesn't take me long to catch up. Grabbing her face, I slanted her head and kissed her back. If she's the sea, I'll happily drown in her.

I kiss her like we're at war.

Biting and sucking on that plump bottom lip, *demanding* entrance. Once she finally opens for me, I groan into her mouth.

God, I've missed her. And I tell her so.

"I've missed you so fucking much Songbird."

I've missed her taste. I've missed her body pressed to mine. I've missed her tenacity. We become a flurry of hands, tongues and teeth. Sliding my hands down her back, I palm her ass, squeezing. It's still so sweet. So tight. Before she has time to protest, I break the kiss and throw her over my shoulder. Once we reach the tailgate, I lower it and set her down gently. After nudging her legs apart with my knees, I step forward so we're chest to chest. Bringing one hand up, I wrap it around her throat, not squeezing, just holding. Then I'm twisting my other fist in her long locks, tilting her head up so she's facing me, needing to see her eyes when I ask my next question.

"Has there been anyone else Sage?"

Her mouth parts on a soft exhale, storm cloud eyes widening. She tries to turn away, but I don't let her. Pulling her hair tighter, she winces, and I dare her to look away from me. When she doesn't, I ask again.

"Sage, has there been anyone else?"

Whispering so low, I almost miss it. She answers. And it's the sweetest fucking thing. "No."

Leaning closer, my lips brush against her ear as I tell her my truth.

"Your memory haunted me for years. *You. Haunted. Me.* I wouldn't betray what we had. *Couldn't betray you.* All this time, I believed death took you. While I'm angry, so very fucking angry that you lied, that you didn't confide in me, *that you left.*" she winces as she tries to pull away again, but I'm not having it, squeezing the hand around her throat tighter in warning before continuing in a growl, "The love I have for you didn't just go away, I've been stuck, never moving forward. There's been no one else, *even in death, I belonged to you.* Now that you're here, I'm not letting you go. If you try to run again, I will chase you and when I catch you, *I'll bend you over my knee before fucking you so hard, you can't walk for a week.*"

When I pulled back, her eyes were glowing.

Oh, Songbird, you like the sound of that don't you?

Wetting her lips, she rasps out, "I've always been yours Dean, I was just waiting for you to catch up."

This infuriating fucking woman.

In a blink, I'm on her. Mouths slamming together violently, she gives as good as she gets. Years of pent-up desire and rage unleash. With a flick of my wrist, I pull out my knife and make quick work of her sweater before ripping it away from her body. There are too many layers, before I can give the shirt she's wearing the same treatment, she catches my wrists gently.

"Please don't, not this one."

Stepping back, I get a better look at the frayed material, the overly washed 'Ravenswood Football' printed on the front, my eyes snap to hers.

"It's the only piece of you I could take with me. I've kept it all this time, I don't want you to cut it. Please. Don't."

It's the 'please' that does me in, the beast in my chest settles and my movements slow. Methodically, I do as she asks and place it gently in the bed of the truck. Once I have her sitting in just a sports bra, I slip it over her head too. Proof that she carried my child shows, faint stretch marks cut a path low on her flat stomach, seeing where my gaze has gone, she tries to cover them.

We're not doing that. Tsking, I pull her fingers away and push her arms out to the side.

"Don't. You're beautiful, Sage. Fucking beautiful. Don't hide from me. Every inch of you is perfection, there's not one part I don't like, no part I don't want to see."

I trail a finger over the silver streaks, and she shudders.

She's the mother of my child, the absolute love of my life. Slowly she brings her arms up, guiding the cut off my shoulders with shaking hands and places it on top of her own clothes. From there I take over, reaching behind my neck I pull my shirt over my head in one fell swoop. Her eyes widen as she maps my body, categorizing each dip and valley, and the tattoos on display. I jolt when she places her hands on me, startled, she goes to snatch them away.

I don't think so.

Quickly grabbing her retreating palms, I put them back on my chest. Hesitantly, she leans forward and kisses my abdomen, working her way down. I'm only capable of letting her explore for a moment before impatience wins out and I'm yanking her head back and taking her lips again.

Reaching between us, I untie the drawstring on her shorts and let her shimmy them off. Stepping back, I remove my own jeans and boots. We're far enough in the woods that no one would see us unless they travel down the dirt road. Running my hands up her legs, she shivers in anticipation. Lowering onto my knees, like a knight before his queen, my tongue trails a path to her inner thigh. Without warning, I bite down, then quickly kiss the sting away as she whimpers, and goes limp, laying back in the truck bed.

I haven't forgotten, my girl likes a bite of pain with her pleasure.

I'm so close to where I want to be, breathing in, it's an inherent need to taste her sweetness. She's so wet for me, all that honey dripping down her thighs. Fuck I've missed this, like a man starved, I part her lips with my thumbs and dive in. Grabbing a fistful of my hair, she bucks into my mouth, I can't tell if she's trying to push me away or pull me closer. With flat swipes of my tongue, I lick her from back to front. Raspy cries of pleasure spur me on, so I go harder, putting more pressure on the swollen bud while pushing two fingers inside, pumping slowly.

When I find that sweet spot, I rub it and curl my fingers while sucking her clit in tandem and she goes off like a rocket, arousal flooding my tastebuds, dripping down my beard. This is what addiction feels like, I never want to stop.

We're on limited time.

Giving her one last swipe with my tongue, one last taste, I palm each side of her waist, dragging her further towards the edge of the truck bed and fill her roughly with a single thrust.

Crying out, her back arches as static fills my head, my vision going white.

She's so fucking tight. I forgot how good this felt.

Unable to contain my thoughts, I growl them out.

"Fucking made for me."

"Mine."

When my vision clears, her mouth is parted in a silent 'o'. I can't move yet. I'm already close, it's been too long; I'm feeling like a teenager again, fighting off my release. Watery eyes finally open as her gaze meets mine. With a smirk, she rolls her hips, challenging me. She knows I'm struggling. She can feel it. This push and pull, damn I've missed it.

"Move Raven, please move." She rasps.

"Are you sure you're ready for it baby?"

When she goes to snark back, I'm lifting her quickly, rosebud nipples scraping my chest as I pull all the way out and slam back in. Powerful snaps of my hips have her perfect tits bouncing against me. Unhinged, I do it again and again until she's right on the brink. Her sweet cunt squeezes me. Sweat slides down my spine as I slip one hand down her back, doing as I imagined in the shower. I wrap her long hair around my fist and use it like a lead rope, pulling her taut, finding that perfect rhythm, I'm barreling into her and my Songbird meets me stroke for stroke.

With a sharp tug on those copper curls, I tilted her neck and bit down on the tender flesh. Relishing the gasp that leaves her lips. Needing more, my arm goes under her knee, lifting her leg higher on my waist, changing the angle. The new fit has her squeezing my cock harder, milking it, her walls start rippling and heat builds. Her next climax is close, I can feel it.

Utter. Perfection.

She moans my name in a breathy exhale. "Dean."

I know I've got her.

"That's it baby, you're taking me so well, your sweet pussy was made to take me." With another harsh thrust, I bottom out and stay there, rasping through clenched teeth, I command, "Come for me Songbird." The last of my control snaps as her walls flutter, her orgasm consumes me, my movements become jerky, no rhythm. Just feeling.

I lose myself to her.

"You're. Mine. All. Mine." Each snarled word is punctuated with a thrust, driving the point home.

"Yes!" She cries out on a sob.

When I finish harder than I ever have in my life, I see stars, galaxies, *the fucking milky way.*

Life altering.

We're both breathing heavily as we come down. When I pull out, still in a trance, I watch enraptured as our combined arousal floods out with me. Like a man possessed, I rub my fingers over her, scooping it up and pushing it back where it belongs. Continuing my ministrations, I can't help but play, bringing her over the edge once more until she's a whimpering mess. When she's boneless, I use my t-shirt to clean between her thighs and help put her clothes back on. Before she can climb back in the truck, I grab her wrist and pull her to me. Holding her face, I kiss her slowly, nothing like the earlier attack. When we finally come up for air, I press our foreheads together.

"From this point forward, total honesty Sage. I need it. I can't lose you again. Not when I've just found you. I'm going to be here for you, for both of you... please, let me." I'm practically begging,

I don't care.

Taking my hand, she kisses the tips of my fingers before murmuring, "Deal."

CHAPTER SEVENTEEN
Sage

I can honestly say this wasn't on my bingo card.

You mean to tell me you weren't expecting to expose your secrets and then get fucked like an animal in the bed of your truck? Maybe not, but you have no regrets.

The drive back to my house wasn't fraught with tension, not like before. We'd not worked out everything, obviously, but there was a new kind of peace between us.

I suppose a good fuck will do that to you and damnnnn if it wasn't good.

Not me over here getting flustered just thinking about it. Tessa would be so proud.

Bursting my own bubble, my brain starts rapid firing, the unanswered questions land like stones, one after another in quick succession, killing my mood.

Where do we go from here?

What does this mean for Jericho?

How do we keep from danger?

What happens when this is all over?

Will he go back to Ravenswood?

Would he want us to go with him?

Before I could voice all that concerned me, we were in my driveway and Dean was leaning over the console, kissing me thoroughly. With a rumbled promise to see me later, he was climbing out of my truck and riding off into the sunset. Leaving me befuddled for a few minutes in the driver's seat.

Once I gathered the strength, I stumbled into my house and towards my ensuite. Just the thought of washing him away hurt, but I desperately needed a hot shower to clear my head. The juncture between my legs was sore, but oh, how delicious a feeling. It's been too long. Tess would say it's like riding a bike, I don't think I agree. In a lot of ways, he's the same. But in others, he's completely different. There's a kind of primal savagery in the way he moves, in the way he speaks. That wasn't there before. Granted, Dean's always been serious and protective, if not a little dark. Now, he's a new beast entirely. The years haven't been easy on him, it's clear to see.

When given the same choice as before, would I do it differently? I'm not sure. I had Jericho to keep me going, who did Dean have? These thoughts plague me as I finish my shower and step into my clothes. It's gotten late. Do I pick up Jericho now, or do I wait until the morning? Pulling out my cell, I text Brad.

Harlow: How was today?

He must not be busy because his reply comes swiftly.

Brad: It was great! They scrimmaged before dinner and now we're doing smores. *image*

Taking in Jeri's marshmallow covered face, I can't help but smile.

I'm not sure how to explain that I'll be picking her up early without Brad asking questions. I've typed and erased a few times before settling on keeping it simple.

Harlow: That's awesome! Unfortunately, I'll have to pick her up tomorrow. I hate to cut camp short, but we've got a family situation, and I need her home for it.

Brad: Is everything okay?

I suppose it does seem strange that I'm pulling her out two days early, not that I owe him any kind of explanation.

Harlow: Everything is fine. Could you make sure she's ready to go in the morning, around 9?

Brad: Sure. Yeah. I can do that. I'm here if you need anything... As a friend of course.

Harlow: Thanks.

Flopping onto my sofa, I closed his thread and pulled up Tessa's.

Harlow: All good at TBC?

If I had to guess, I'd say she's most definitely busy. Not only am I off work this week, but it's ladies' night. Snorting to myself, I think about Donnie being there for that.

I'm sure he's loving it.

Although now that I think about it, he seems to have his eye on my friend. Turning on my tv, I scroll mindlessly through Netflix while waiting for her response. Not finding anything of interest, I select a true crime documentary and meander towards my kitchen to pour a glass of wine.

As I'm cozying back onto the sectional, my phone pings.

Tessa: Define good?

That's not cryptic.

Harlow: Nobody's hurt, nothing's on fire, there's no liquor shortage... Ya know the basic levels of not goodness for a bar?

Tessa: Well, none of those things are happening. Would you like me to show you what is?

Harlow: I'm intrigued...

Tessa: *video*

A 30 second clip of a shirtless, *verrrry chiseled Donnie*, surrounded by screaming women as he dances on stage, 'coyote ugly' style to a *Shania Twain* song fills my phone screen. He's grinning suggestively while looking at the camera. Pointing at whoever's recording -I assume it's Tessa- he winks and runs his tongue over his teeth. Almost spitting my wine from laughing, I managed to reign it in but swallowed down the wrong pipe. A few choking gasps later, I wipe my watering eyes and text her back.

Harlow: WTF is he doing????

Tessa: Embracing ladies' night to the fullest?

Harlow: And you're just letting him?

Tessa: I told him he wasn't sexy.... He's proving a point.

Harlow: .... *smh emoji*

Tessa: I know! Okay! Dios Mio. I know the man is sex candy. But... I'm immune.

Harlow: Sweet Jesus Tessie. You're immune? Are you, are you really? How may abs does the man have?

Tessa: Shut up. You know nothing Jon Snow. Besides, he's leaving now. Some young pup came to replace him, to the detriment of all the ladies present. Also... *eyes emoji* He has eight. I counted. How does one get abs on their ribs? I'm asking for a friend.

Harlow: You can lie to yourself, but never me babe. What was it you said, LET THE MAN EAT YOU. Sounds like you should take your own advice. Might do you some good.

Tessa: I will not. What's good for the hole isn't always good for the soul. You can take that advice to the bank.

What's good for the? Is she serious?

There have been quite a few 'face palm' moments throughout our friendship, this is one of them. My phone pings again, I'm almost afraid to look.

Tessa: Speaking of letting a man eat you, did you? *eyes emoji*

I absolutely cannot with her.

Harlow: Don't you have work to do?

Tessa: Was it at least good? He's got the energy too. *eggplant emoji*

Harlow: I don't kiss and tell.

Tessa: You don't kiss.

Tessa: LOL. That's ok mami, just wait, I'll get it out of you. *detective emoji* It's getting rowdy in here. I think these women are trying to eat the new kid. Gtg save the day. *kisses*

Flinging my cell towards the end of the couch, I polish off my wine. This time when I go to refill, I don't bother using a glass, I bring the whole bottle back to the living room with me. I was right when I went shopping, I do need it.

CHAPTER EIGHTEEN
Dean

Church started when Donnie finally graced us with his presence. He sauntered into the meeting room with a cocky smile on his face. Taking his seat beside me, it fell away, eyes taking on a hard edge. It was time to get down to business. Looking from left to right, I took in the Saints MC brothers, all wearing similar expressions. Petey sat at the head of the table across from me and at my nod, he banged his gavel.

"Dean Graham has news. Everyone pay attention."

Petey finished his call to order and waved for me to take over, the floor was mine. The question is, where should I begin?

Donnie, reading my mind stage whispered, "From the beginning, D. One thing at time."

With no other choice, I start sharing.

"For those unfamiliar with me, I'm Aberdean Graham, VP and club fixer for the Ravens MC. Yesterday, Donnie and I paid a visit to The Black Cat, I'm sure you locals are familiar with the place. We paid a visit at the behest of the Ravens Prez, my father. He'd heard rumor that the traffic wasn't what you'd call 'friendly'." I gestured to my brother, "Donnie and I saw what we believed to be two bratva members visiting the establishment. Now I'll admit, I got distracted while there, you see eight years ago, my old lady died." Grabbing my glass of beer, I hold up a finger, asking for just a moment while taking a long drink.

Setting the glass back down, I continue.

"Except, while we were there, so was she. My woman was very much alive and on stage singing."

Jorge interrupts me, "How is this relevant?"

Donnie barks impatiently, "He's getting to the point. The man just had his life changed drastically, slow your roll friend."

"Enough." Petey booms out, "Dean, take your time. Tell us what all this means."

Playing with the condensation on my glass I answer quietly, but not meekly, "My girl faked her death, because of Mihailo Medvedev. The man was planning to use my girl against Colin McGregor and take over his territories. She was his collateral."

Petey chimes in again, I suppose it doesn't make much sense without the big-ticket fact.

"Why is she so important to Mihailo? Who is she Dean?"

I catch Donnie's eye, and he winces sympathetically. We both know I'd rather not share this, but to keep Sage safe I have to. It's time for the truth to come out. As much as I begrudge Thorne's reasoning all those years ago, I understand it. In the grand scheme of things, it was more helpful for the bureau than anyone else. I'm not a trigger-happy kid anymore. While I'm still full of inner demons and prone to violence, I'm smarter about it (for the most part). My hot head nature would have gotten me killed years ago. Now, I'm ready to play the long game.

With a deep inhale, I breathe out the truth.

"She's Colin McGregor's daughter."

Jaws drop one by one as the table goes speechless.

After a few moments, the words sink in and Petey clears his throat, "How do we know for sure?"

"I don't have all the details yet. But believe me, she's his daughter. My contact with the bureau will be here in two days. He'll inform me of the specifics. For now, I'd prefer it if the information didn't leave this room. I'd like to be the one to tell Colin myself. She's my girl, if anyone's going to play messenger, it's me."

Jorge bursts out laughing from beside Petey, "He'll kill you."

Petey chimes in, his voice hard. "He won't."

Donnie asks hesitantly, my brother is afraid for me, "What makes you so sure?"

Petey levels my brother with a look, "The man may be deranged, but if your girl is his daughter, he won't kill you, simply because she loves you. My father dealt with Colin a lot through the years; I've talked to the man. Watched him. It's what I do. I watch people. You can learn a lot when you take the time. Colin -though he is deranged- he's a family man. He loves his daughter fiercely. Her picture is still above the mantle in his compound living room. If she loves you, he won't kill you. The question is, does she?"

I rub under my beard, touching her mark on my skin. I know how I feel about her, I'm almost positive she still feels the same. She hasn't said it, but she doesn't have to make some great proclamation.

In my soul I know.

"She does. I'm sure."

Petey nods, "Then you'll be fine. He may fuck you up for claiming her," his lip tips up at the corner, "but he won't kill you."

Holding up a hand, "There's one more thing."

Jorge asks with an eyeroll, "You got another secret heir we don't know about?"

I laugh sardonically, I'm really not liking this guy, "Actually, yeah. Mine. Colin has a granddaughter. My girl found out she was pregnant after she ran. Jericho is seven. She'll need to be protected."

Petey stares at me for a moment, weighing my words and their implications. Jorge wasn't far off; Jericho is a child, but an heir to the Irish Brotherhood regardless. He sees the steel in my gaze. This request is nonnegotiable.

"Your daughter will have the Saints protection. Have you informed Angus?"

My brother looks at me then, we've already discussed this. With a shrug of his shoulders, he's giving me permission to clue everyone else in.

"Donnie and I seem to think our Prez already knows. Jora found out through our bureau contact; he went to him after my girl received a threat delivered on her porch. Chances are, if Jora knows, he's already informed Pops. Jora's loyal to me, but he's loyal to the club even if he's not a patched member. My father likely knows and is just waiting for me to decide how to play this. I'll call him after church concludes, one thing at a time."

Petey rubs his chin with his thumb and forefinger, taking in everything I've said quietly. We wait in stilted silence for him to gather his thoughts. Finally, he speaks. "We're going to put a protection detail on your woman and child, along with continuing to guard our warehouses for the next two days. At that point, I'm not comfortable keeping this from Colin. You need to understand, if he finds out my club knew and didn't come forward, he'll burn it to the ground. Two days Dean, I'll give you enough time for your bureau contact to arrive, then we'll hold church again. I think it's only fair we all know what he knows. You agree?"

"I do. It's time Colin knew the truth, but I don't want to give it to him halfway, I want all the facts first."

Ultimately, this was what I was hoping for.

"Does anyone else have anything for tonight?"

When no one else chimed in, Petey banged his gavel and dismissed us. Donnie and I waited in our seats for everyone to shuffle out. When it was just Petey left. I picked up my empty glass and made my way over to the bar cart across the room. There was something I'd been meaning to ask.

Pouring whiskey, I did just that. "Pete, why did you ask for me?"

"What do you mean?"

"My Pops said you'd asked for the club fixer. I want to know why? You're a levelheaded guy. Other than the first night, you've proven that since I've been here. So, why am I here?"

When I turn around to face him, he's twirling a pen between his fingers.

"Truth is, I don't want to be President, never did, I was grandfathered in. Those men out there, while some of them are decent, none of them have leadership qualities."

Taking a sip of my drink, I settled back in my seat.

"That doesn't really answer my question."

Tossing the pen across the table, "Truthfully. I wanted to see your mettle. This is probably coming out of left field, but I'd like to elect you for the Prez position... here. I've been talking with Angus about it, he knew beforehand, already cleared it with Colin. The Saints is a small chapter. Your father and I have been working out terms, make it a Ravens sister charter. We'd change colors and the Raven's would take ownership as well as responsibility of the guys. I'd like to stay on as a brother, but I don't want to lead. I respect the Ravens and what they stand for... also, I respect you."

My brother cuts in with clear disbelief, "You mean, you want Dean to move down here and take over this club? And Pop's is okay with this?"

Petey nods stoically, "Yes. That's exactly what I'm saying. Seems to me, he's got a reason to stay now, two of them in fact."

"Do any of the brothers here know about your plans?"

"They do. We voted on it before I reached out to Angus. There was only one who didn't want change."

"Let me guess, Jorge?"

Petey nods. That doesn't surprise me, he's not been exactly pleasant since we arrived. It's nothing I can't handle. This will take some thought. I wasn't prepared and I still need to speak with my father. Leaving Ravenswood would be no hardship, I'm rarely there as it stands. Pete's right though, I do have two reasons to be here, once I talk to my Pop's, I need to talk to Sage. *That's assuming Colin doesn't kill me.* Here's to hoping.

Pete cuts into my thoughts, "Take the next few days and think it over, until you decide, we can wait. I'm sure there are a few things you'll need to discuss with your old man, and your girl."

Clearing my throat, "Yeah, there are."

Rapping his knuckles on the table, he rises from his seat and grabs a bottle of bourbon from the bar cart. As he reaches the door, he looks over his shoulder. "If you decide yes, I would like to stay on as a Raven. I've always been better in the shadows. Gathering intel is my strong suit, I'd make a good spy master for you. If you need something in the meantime, come find me."

With that last parting remark, he shoulders his way out to drown in the bottle.

My brother and I stared at each other for a few minutes before I pulled out my phone to call our father. The line rings twice and we hear a gruff 'Yeah'.

Donnie greets him, "Hey Pops, when were you going to tell

Deanie weenie you wanted to send him away? Do you not love him anymore? I always knew I was the favorite."

I roll my eyes at my brother's antics and can imagine my father doing the same.

He scoffs, "Don, you idiot. I didn't want to send him away... and if we're talking favorites, it's obviously Knox. He's the least bit of trouble outta the three of you. But the offer is a good one, he'd have his space, hell, he never wants to be here anyway. Thought it'd be a fresh start for him. Contrary to what you all think, I do give a shit about my sons and want them to be happy. Ravenswood wasn't that for Aberdean, I mean, fuck, he just held a gun to Vick's head the other day. I had to have Jora track her down and force her to sign an NDA. The damn girl only agreed because I let her back in the clubhouse. This place isn't good for his mental health."

"Please, do continue having a conversation about me like I'm not right here."

My father finally addresses me without missing a beat, "Hello son, how are you? Jora says Sage looks good for a dead woman. Oh, how's my granddaughter?"

Donnie barks out a laugh and I growl at him.

Fucking Jora, I knew it.

"I'm not sure yet. Haven't met her. She's beautiful though, I can send you a pic. Sage looks incredible. Jora needs to shut the fuck up and keep his thoughts to himself. Also, thanks for calling to check on me. You give a shit you say? Would have been nice to hear from my Pop's when he found out, not when I called."

My father laughs obnoxiously, "You're a grown man, I figured you'd reach out when you needed to talk. Is that what this is? Need to talk to your old man? A long-distance hand holding?"

He's exasperating, "I need to talk about Colin. If you know all that I do, then you know I'm between a rock and a rock with him."

Sighing dramatically, he answers me. "Colin is going to lose his mind when he finds out. You'll have to make sure Petey keeps a fire extinguisher on hand, the devil loves to burn things… oh and hide all the sharp objects, it might be best if you walk around in a bulletproof vest for a while. You did knock up his daughter." At that, Donnie let's out a pained whine, my father hears it.

Dad chuckles, "Don't worry Donal, we've got your brother's back. You hear me Aberdean? I've got you. I'm coming down with Jora and Thorne."

Donnie perks up, "I knew you missed us, but damn Pops, you're getting up there, can you handle that long of a ride these days?"

"I can still kick your ass kiddo; don't you forget it."

My brother and father bickered back and forth for a while, leaving me out of it and lost in thought.

Should I be more afraid than I am? Probably.

With my father involved, I can't bring myself to be. Like he said, I'm a grown man, but something about having my father's support makes me feel invincible.

Which is stupid. But it means the world to me.

Colin can't kill me; I've got too much to live for. My girls need me, and I plan to be there for them no matter what. If that means standing up to the don of the Irish Brotherhood, I will do that. If it means moving here, I'll do that too.

Sage is at home, that's where I want to be.

Slicing my hand through the air, I cut off my brother, "Don, you can call Pop's from your cell if you want to continue this riveting conversation, I've got someone waiting on me."

With a boisterous laugh, my father disconnects and a few moments later, Donnie's phone rings. On that note, I drain my glass and head to the person I want to see most.

CHAPTER NINETEEN
Sage

It's late when I feel someone squeeze into bed, my first instinct is to panic but then the smell of leather and mint hit me. A strong arm bands around my waist, and I turn into him. The moonlight casts a soft glow, highlighting Dean as he's propped up on an elbow, looking down at me. It's a beautiful sight, one a girl could get used to.

Hope is a butterfly in my chest, wanting that. Always wanting that.

He must take my silence as apprehension, murmuring quietly, he asks, "Is this, okay?"

"It is." snuggling further into his hold, I leaned forward and pressed a kiss to his bare chest. He's like a furnace, lifting the blanket, I see he's in boxers and nothing else.

"I didn't want to spend a night away."

Giggling into his pectorals, it reminds me of the nights he used to climb onto the balcony and sneak into my bedroom. "Just like old times."

Chuckling quietly, he presses his face into my hair and kisses my forehead softly.

"Sleep Songbird. We'll talk in the morning." On that final note, he relaxes deeper into the mattress, one arm under my pillow, the other still wrapped around me.

With him this close, my body wakes up full force. My mind starts racing and the heat radiating off him spreads throughout my limbs, settling low in my gut. Sparks zing from the contact. Now that he's here, I can't get enough. Twisting around so my back to his chest, I start shifting my hips, rocking them slowly. Dean's hand spreads out on my ribcage, fingers squeezing slightly.

His voice is raspy, "What do you need Sage?"

I keep going as I answer breathlessly, "You."

"Do you need help sleeping baby?"

"Please."

Without another word, Dean slowly drifts his hands to my pajama bottoms. I'm thanking earlier me for having the forethought to go without panties. Settling his arm under my neck, he tugs so we're flush. So close I feel his erection digging into my backside. Fingers inch under the elastic waistband on a southbound mission. Lifting one leg, he wedges his knee between mine. Letting my leg drop, I drape it over his thigh, spreading myself wider to grant him access. His fingers finally find my folds, at the first brush against me, I hiss. I'm so unbelievably wet, this can't be normal.

Suppressing myself for years probably isn't healthy.

Dean rubs back and forth in slow, tantalizing strokes, touching everywhere but my clit. When I'm panting from anticipation, he finally gives me what I need and pinches my swollen bud between his fingers. Taking his time as he rolls it back and forth. I'm so close but I need more.

At this point, I'm not above begging.

"More, please, I need more."

Lowering his mouth to my ear, he scrapes his teeth across my lobe and whispers hoarsely, "Touch yourself Songbird, show me how you do it, let me watch you play with that pretty pussy."

He doesn't have to tell me twice; I don't hesitate to bring my hand down and replace his fingers with my own. After the first flick of my wrist, Dean shoves two fingers inside me. Pumping them in and out, matching my movements. It's so fucking hot, so sensual. We've been here before, but this feels new. Like we're learning each other all over again. Hips rolling into him, I'm on a collision course, the orgasm is right at the tip of my fingers, he picks up his pace and adds a third, stretching me so well, hitting that sweet spot *just right.*

"Yesmygodyesssss." My words come out a garbled moan into the night.

Moving the arm that's under my neck, he pulls my tank top down and pinches my nipple, rolling and tugging on the hardened tip as he bites my shoulder *hard.*

That does it folks, I explode.

Rough words of encouragement rumble in my ear, "Give it to me Songbird, I want all of it."

My body is moving of its own volition, ass grinding into his erection, he groans and rocks with me. Skin covered in a sheen of sweat, I turn to face him, planning to return the favor. As I move, he pulls his fingers from me and brings them to his mouth. I watch, mouth gaping, as he licks each digit slowly, moaning as if he's savoring the flavor. Snapping out of it, I reach for his boxers, but he grabs my wrist, halting me. Never breaking eye contact, he pulls the hand I used to touch myself to his mouth and draws my fingers between his lips, sucking them clean.

One. By. One.

When he's finished, I try to touch him again, but he shakes his head, still denying me.

At the furrow in my brow, he murmurs, "Songbird, if you wander down there, you'll find I've already finished." My mouth pops open, and he gently closes it, "I'm not ashamed to admit, it's been eight years. I'm going to be quick on the draw until we get used to this again -and believe me when I say, we will be getting used to this- that's a promise. You have no idea how sexy you are when you orgasm. I could watch it all the time, *and I do plan to*. But not now, tonight, we need sleep. This isn't a tit for tat kind of relationship. Plus, there are things to discuss in the morning and a little girl to pick up. Now, I'm going to use your bathroom to clean the oyster in my shorts and you're going to fall asleep sated. Understood?"

Looking in his eyes, I can see he means business, when I don't protest, he leans forward whispering against my temple, "Good girl."

Pressing a kiss to my forehead, he climbs from the bed.

He's right, I'm asleep before I know it and it's the best damn sleep I've gotten in years.

Waking before Dean gives me the opportunity to really take in the details I've missed. Chest down on the mattress, I gently trace the tattoos covering his back and shoulders. He really is a walking canvas. Long black hair covers his face, I'd love nothing more than to move it and continue my creeping, but nature calls. Easing myself from the bed, I head into the bathroom and do my business. When I walked back into my room, he was still asleep, only now, he pulled my pillow to his face and snuggled in. As quietly as possible, I grabbed my cell and snapped a picture. The sheets cover him from the waist down, but with his strong back on display, it's a glorious photo. Making my way to the laundry room, I grabbed a fresh sports bra from the basket and a pair of biker shorts. After changing in my living room, I set about my morning routine.

I've just hit four miles on my treadmill when a throat clears behind me. Slowing down, I turn to find Dean leaning across the door frame, arms crossed.

Looking so delicious it should be illegal.

He's barefoot and bare chested, in just a pair of low-slung jeans. His hair is wild from sleep and black curls brush against his collar bones. When I'm at a walking pace, he pushes from the door and makes his way towards me. Glancing down at the machine, he arches a brow, impressed.

"Not too shabby Songbird. Do you usually go more?"

I'm breathless, but it's not from running. "Five miles first thing in the morning. Then coffee and a shower. Today, we'll have to get coffee to-go. But the shower? It can't wait."

Bringing his thumb up, he drags it down his plump bottom lip, looking at me through lowered lashes, a mischievous grin on his face. "No, you're right. The shower can't wait."

His smile dazzles, before I know what's happening, he's scooping me over his shoulder, I grab the waistband of his jeans to stabilize myself and swat his perfect ass. *This is becoming a habit.* He laughs loudly while he shuts my treadmill down. Then he's making his way to my bathroom with me slung like a bale of hay. Water sounds from the hallway, he's already started the shower. When we arrive, he sits me on the sink and makes quick work of my bra and tennis shoes. Ushering me to stand, he peels my biker shorts down and gasps when he sees I'm not wearing any underwear.

Shrugging, I bat my eyes innocently, "What? I knew I was going to shower, so I didn't waste a pair."

"Get in the water you dirty little Songbird."

Swaying my hips a little more than usual, I do as I'm told. Dunking my head under the spray, I watch through the glass door as he peels his own jeans and boxers off. Opening the door, he climbs in behind me.

Reaching for shampoo, Dean snatches the bottle from me, "Let me."

I'm not sure he understands how much hair I have, in challenge I say, "Go for it."

Arching a brow, he does just that.

He's methodical as he completes his task, working his way down from my roots and gently rubbing the ends. When he's satisfied, he turns me around and diligently rinses the suds away. Repeating the same process with my conditioner. It's heavenly, I can't help but moan. When he goes to do his own hair, I make the attempt to return the favor, but he's so much taller than me, it proves impossible. At my pout, he chuckles. Not to be deterred, I grab a loofa, lather it and start in on his body. He finishes rinsing conditioner from his own hair and then places his hand over mine. Our bodies are soapy, pressed together. When I catch sight of Dean's pupils, the black is almost eating the silver entirely as he looks me up and down, cataloging each curve and valley. Dropping the loofa, I shrug my shoulders in an 'oopsie daisy' fashion and use my hands to rub the soap into his skin, never breaking his stare, I watch his expression grow hungrier and hungrier.

Fucking finally, he snaps, Dean spins me around quickly and places my hands on the wall, rumbling a warning against my back, "This will be quick."

Pushing my ass back into his cock, he groans as I respond, "Just fuck me Dean."

Barreling me against the tiled wall, he fists my hair and rails into me with a punishing thrust.

"*Fuuuuuuuck yes,* Songbird, already so wet, this is my perfect pussy."

There's no hesitation this time, no warmup. Slamming into me like a tidal wave, he keeps the same punishing pace. In no time at all, I'm on the precipice. His arms are so long, he's completely wrapped around me, hips snapping against mine. My arms give out and my nipples scrape against the cool tile, but I don't mind the delicious friction. Slipping my arm around his neck, I pull his face down to mine. He kisses me deeply and I moan into his mouth, letting him swallow the sound whole.

Breaking away, he growls against my lips, "Come for me Songbird."

It's like he's got his finger on the trigger. When he says do it, my body listens.

I come so hard so fast, it knocks the wind from me. A few pumps later and he's climaxing too. Hot jets of him fill me and I *relish it*. Pumping slowly, we ride the wave together before he gently places kiss along my shoulder, and we take turns cleaning up again.

Leaving the bathroom wrapped in a towel, I make my way to my dresser and notice what I didn't earlier. There's a small duffel bag next to my closet. When he comes out towel slung around his waist, I short circuit-*if he keeps walking around like this, I'm going to have a coronary*- then I ask about it.

"Did you have this last night?"

Pulling a change of clothes from the bag, he answers, "No. Donnie dropped it off while you were running a marathon. He drove a cage, so you probably didn't hear him pull up."

"Oh okay," it's probably a stupid question, but I ask anyway, "you plan on staying here, right?"

He chuckles, "Songbird. That's what the bag is for. You're good with that, yes?"

"Of course I am! I want you here, I just worry about Jeri. Do you feel comfortable being here with her?"

Dropping what's in his hands, he sits on the edge of my bed and watches me. Concern lining his brow. "Do you feel comfortable with Jeri knowing who I am? What have you even told her?"

I finish pulling on my sundress and sit down beside him.

Taking his hand, I look him in the eye, not liking what I'm seeing.

"I told her a story."

"What story?" His gaze drops to our hands.

"About the Songbird and the Raven."

"You told her our story?"

"Kind of, just listen." Fiddling with my fingers, he does. "I told her the Raven loved the Songbird so much and she loved him too, it was the greatest kind of love, the forever kind. One day, some hunters came, they chased the Songbird, and she was scared. When they weren't looking, the Songbird had to fly away, she hid from them, but she also hid from the Raven, breaking his heart to keep him safe. You see, the hunters would have hurt him, and she couldn't live with that. After a while, the Songbird learned the Raven had left her a gift, *a gift he didn't know about*. A baby bird in her belly. I told her one day the Raven would find them, and he'd stay." He continues playing with my fingers, not making eye contact.

Lifting his chin, I finish softly, "She asked me one day, probably two years ago, if I was the Songbird and if her daddy was the Raven. I said yes, her daddy was like the darkest night, the strongest of ravens and that one day, we would be together. One day, he would find us. Naturally, she wanted to know why you weren't here now. I told her that you would come when the time was right, it's something she's been looking forward to."

Stroking his chin, I kiss him softly. Dean throws his arms around me, and we just sit, soaking each other in for a moment before pulling away and getting ready to get our girl.

Her Raven's come home.

CHAPTER TWENTY
Sage

Dean's hand stayed on my thigh the entire drive to camp. Since we finally broke through our barriers, it's like he can't help himself. If he's around, he touches me. I absolutely do not mind it. The warmth of his palm was comforting as my anxiety increased each mile we drew closer to Jericho. Pulling through the gate and to the admin building, my chest tightened. This was it. She was going to meet him for the first time. Removing his hand, he brought his fingers to the nape of my neck and rubbed the tension filled area in firm circles.

"We don't have to tell her yet. Let's just say I'm a friend."

Turning as much as his hand on my neck would allow, I viewed him from my peripheral, noting the concern in his expression.

I laughed lightly, "She won't believe that. I don't bring new people around her and there have been no men. The girl is perceptive, she'll know something is up. It's better to be honest. Let's focus on getting her in the truck and we'll take her to get some lunch and talk... if that even works."

"What do you mean?" His brows furrow, forming a 'v' between them.

Pulling his hand away, he leans back in his seat and looks at the camp site. It's a newly renovated area, the administration building is next to the mess hall, a large fire pit stands in the middle of the square. Ten cabins in a row are off to the side. Through the tree line, a trail leads to an open field and beyond that, a small lake with a large dock that houses kayaks and canoes.

My eyes follow where he's looking before I blow out an exasperated breath, "It's just, Jeri is something else entirely. I mean it when I say she's perceptive. She's like a mini detective, little gets by her. If she starts in before we make it to the truck, well... you'll see."

"Do you want me to come with you?"

Shaking my head, I paused before getting out of the truck. "I don't think that's necessary. I'm hoping she'll come quicker if she doesn't see you. I'd rather not do this here; she'll start in on the questions, I'd rather have her in the truck before that."

Noticing movement, I look up to see Brad walking out of the admin building, heading our way.

With my hand on the door handle, Dean stills and asks in a low rumble, "Who is that?"

Do I detect a hint of jealousy?

"That's Brad. He's Jeri's best friend's dad, he's also one of the coaches, he brought the girls."

Brad continues his trek to me, hand raised in greeting and smiling brightly. When he looks over, noticing I'm not alone, his steps falter and his smile drops slightly before he presses on, moving at a more leisurely pace. Trying to catch him before he gets too close, I climb out, as my door shuts, I hear the passenger side shut too.

Well, shit.

Squeezing my eyes tightly, I send up a silent prayer that Dean doesn't go 'agressy' and 'possessy'. Brad's a sap, poor guy, doesn't stand a chance.

Rounding the truck, Dean comes to stand at my side, placing a hand on my lower back and guiding me forward. When he reaches us, there's a question on Brad's face. Eyes moving, taking in the hand at my back, the way we're positioned so close together, and his lips purse.

Dean might as well piss on me.

Tired of being a sideshow attraction, I clear my throat, snapping him out of it. Regaining his charming smile, he holds out a hand for Dean to shake. I'm thanking my lucky stars that Dean went without his cut today, that's only more fuel for the fire. I don't need the guy asking questions that would only serve to hurt him.

I think back to when Dean and I finished dressing earlier.

Picking his cut up, he regards it for a moment before carefully folding it back into his bag.

"You're not going to wear it today?"

He shook his head at me, "No, not for this. I want to meet her as her dad, not the Ravens VP. Plus, I think it would lead to more questions, today, I just want to talk to her without diving into all of it. Is that okay?"

Honestly, I kind of love that he's deferring to me about her. I know he'll do right by our daughter. He shouldn't worry so much. Striding across the room I throw my arms around him and kiss his bearded jaw. "It's going to be fine, don't worry so much baby."

Distracted by my thoughts, I almost miss the men introducing themselves.

"Hi, I'm Brad, Harlow's neighbor." Brad grins at my Raven as he shakes his hand. Dean's grip must be firm, *a little too firm*, there's a slight wince before Brad clears it away and schools his expression.

Dean gives a megawatt smile in return. He's enjoying this entirely too much.

"I'm Dean. I've recently returned to my girls. It's great that you've been able to help. I appreciate it more than you could know."

Brad nods nervously, "Oh, you're welcome?" He glances at me before tilting his head to the side, mulling over Dean's words.

Dean laughs coyly, rubbing a hand across his neck with a boyish smirk, "Forgive me, I suppose I should've mentioned, I'm Jericho's father."

This man. This ridiculous man.

Looking at me, Dean gives me an impish grin. Inhaling a centering breath, I gather the patience to deal with what is sure to be a dick swinging contest.

Brad could catch flies with the way his jaw has gone lax, looking at me he finally asks on a stutter, "F-father? I didn't know her father was still alive."

That throws me for a loop, I ask, genuinely curious, "Why would you think that?"

Taking a step back, Brad crosses his arms over his chest and shakes his head. "I suppose I just assumed, that's on me. It's just, well you've literally never mentioned him."

Dean cuts in, "You have in-depth conversations, do you?"

Poor Brad sputters, "W-well, no. S-she just... I mean, we're friends?"

"Are you asking or telling? I'm confused." The amusement Dean's feeling over playing with his food his abundantly clear.

Hoping to put him out of his misery, I interrupt and start to position myself between them. "It's fine. I've never mentioned her dad because he's been away until now."

Then Brad does something *truly stupid*. He gets an idea and runs with it. "Ohhhhh." He looks Dean up and down, taking in his long hair and the tattoos that run from his neck to his fingers. Clear judgement flashing in his hazel eyes. Lowering his voice, "What were you in for?"

Lord, strike me down. Strike. Me. Down. This man did not just ask that?

Dean's smile morphs into a baring of his teeth. Through half lowered lids he runs his tongue across his pearly whites and sucks on one of them. Dragging a hand across his beard, he widens his stance and cocks his head, expression growing dark.

"You know, if I *were* fresh out of prison, it wouldn't be polite, or even *smart*, to ask me what I was in for... I mean, would you really want to know? Say, if it was for disemboweling a man? Or ripping out someone's throat with my bare hands, is that something you want to be thinking about... *neighbor*?"

Brad gulps so hard you can hear it, gesturing to one of the far cabins. "You know, I think I'll just go grab Jeri. She was packing the last of her things, should be done by now. Y-you just, uh, wait here."

Dean's eyes never deviate from Brad's retreating form, reminding me of a hawk, circling his prey. Reaching over, I punched his arm.

Rubbing it with a pout, he cuts his eyes at me. "What was that for?"

Crossing my arms over my chest, I lean against the side of my truck and scold him. "You know what it was for, I thought we agreed you'd stay in the vehicle."

Kicking dirt with the toe of his boot, he mumbles like a child, reminding me very much of his daughter, "We never *really* agreed. 'Humphrey Bogart' interrupted us before we could... The man wants you."

Scoffing dramatically, I decide I'm not dignifying that with a response. Taking my position as an invitation, he advances toward me, moving smoother than I thought possible for his size. "Am I wrong?"

Arms come to either side of my waist, caging me in. With his chest pressed against mine, I answer, "No," I huff indignantly, "You're not wrong, the thing is, I don't want him, and he knows it too." I try to look around him, waiting for Jeri to pop out through the doors, but he catches my chin in his hand.

"He's your neighbor?"

I nod, smirking, "Well, he's *our neighbor*, if you want to get technical. Aren't you staying with me for the foreseeable future?"

Leaning in, he drags his lips back and forth across the pulse point in my neck, his beard scraping my skin, before whispering in my ear. "Does he live close enough to hear me fucking you? Would that send the message you think? Or should I try harder? I've not had to opportunity to really take my time and make you sing, but we're going to change that. You're mine Songbird."

This shouldn't be making me wet, but it is. Every dark promise sets my blood aflame and each nerve on edge. He knows how his words affect me, his pupils dilate, and he grits his jaw. My chest goes crimson, the blush travelling slowly up my neck and into my cheeks. Panting softly, I'm trying to hold back a moan. When he leans down and scrapes his teeth across my shoulder, my effort is in vain, an involuntary whimper slips free. I can feel his erection grinding against my hip. A hand starts to wind around my waist, but I'm broken from the spell when I hear my girl shout. "Mom!"

Pulling away from Dean, I shake off the pheromones and take off in a sprint, meeting her halfway. Dropping her bag, she jumps straight into me like a freight train. Arms band around my neck and her little legs wrap around my stomach. Covering her in kisses, I don't stop until she's giggling breathlessly and begging me to stop.

"Did you miss me Jeri girl? I won't let you go until you admit you did."

She groans into my neck, before pulling back and giving me that dimpled smile I love so much, "You know I did momma. Can we go home now?"

Laughing through a nod, I set her on her feet. Taking hold of her hand, I grabbed her bag off the ground. We were heading back towards my truck when Jeri halted suddenly. Her silver eyes went wide, and her mouth popped open. Dean stands in front of the passenger door, hands in his pockets, fidgeting. The two of them are staring at each other like they're in a Mexican standoff. His face is the softest I've ever seen it and the column of his throat works up and down. If I didn't know any better, I'd say he was fighting back tears.

Jeri breaks from the spell first. Looking up at me and then to him, she moves forward slowly, squeezing my hand tightly. Approaching as if he's a wild animal, and she can sense his 'otherness'. When we're three feet from the truck, she pulls from me and does something completely unexpected.

My girl throws herself at him, arms going around his waist as she hugs him tightly. Dropping the bag with a gasp, my hands cover my mouth.

This is surreal.

It catches him off guard too, he's slack jawed. Finally, after what seems like eternity, he moves. Winding his hands under her armpits, he lifts her to him. She looks so tiny against his massive frame. Her body is shaking, I can't tell whether she's crying or laughing.

Dean runs a tattooed hand across her back, soothing her tremors. Leaning in, he nuzzles her hair, breathing in her essence. Pulling back slightly, I finally make out the tears sliding down her freckled face. But... She's smiling. Lifting her hands, she sets them on his cheeks, then trails a finger along his nose and then taps his nose ring. Learning his face, just as he does her. Dean sighs in contentment, closing his eyes briefly and letting her continue her examination. Twirling a long black curl around her finger, Jericho finally speaks.

"You're the Raven." Twisting in his hold, she looks at me, "Mom, he's the Raven."

I'm so beyond words, my throat is thick with emotion. I can only nod in response to what she's said. Scrambling out his arms, she grabs his hand in hers. Looking all the way up, she asks, "You're coming with us, right? Momma said the Raven would come one day."

My girl is so tiny standing next to his towering frame. Dean squats down to her level, his voice garbled, "You know, your mom said you were very smart Jericho. She was right." He tugs on one of her curls too before smiling affectionately, "I am the Raven and I'd very much like to come home, would that be okay with you?"

She snorts a laugh, not looking for my permission. "It's about dang time! You know I'm seven now? Geesh, you've got lots of catching up to do."

He laughs wholeheartedly at that, and it's the most beautiful sound I've ever heard.

CHAPTER TWENTY-ONE
Dean

We decided to stop for burgers along the way back to Sage's place. The entire drive, Jeri wouldn't take her eyes off me as she told us about her time spent at camp. When we climbed from the truck to eat, she hurried around to my side and grabbed my fingers. This little girl had me wrapped around hers, she had me feeling more at peace than I'd ever been. If I thought Sage's name was written on my heart before, it was small potatoes compared to love I already felt for Jericho. Swinging our arms back and forth, she skipped alongside me as we walked across the parking lot. When I reached the door and held it open, she insisted on helping too. We stood there; hands clasped as we opened the door for her mom. After Sage passed by us, Jeri smiled at me, dimples on full display. She's the cutest child I've ever seen.

"Did you know your eyes are the same color as mine?"

Squeezing her fingers, I motioned for her to walk in front of me as I answered. "I did know, but I think yours are much prettier."

"Mom says they're magic, did you know that?"

Shaking my head, I pretend to think hard about what she's said. "I didn't know that, would you tell me?"

Excitedly, she does. "Yes! Silver –that's the color of our eyes in case you didn't know- protects against evil. That's why people wear silver necklaces and stuff. It's a protector color."

Taking my seat beside her, the waitress pops over, when she sees me, she puffs her chest up as she passes out menus, giving me a salacious look. I have no interest in any of that. "Can I get you anything to start, anything at all?"

Ignoring her question for now, I turn to Sage, catching her staring at the waitress, disgust on her face. When her eyes finally meet mine, I wink at her, and she blushes.

She's jealous.

"What do you girls want to drink?"

Jeri asks for chocolate milk and Sage asks for sweet tea. The waitress takes their order, and I let her know I'll just have water before she trudges away. At the insistent tug on my sleeve, I look at my daughter before she asks, "How are you so tall?" Sage chuckles quietly, face hidden behind her menu.

Smiling slyly, I answer my curious seven-year-old, "It's because I ate all the good foods my mom made growing up."

Jeri ponders this, "Huh." then turning to Sage, "You make good food mom, will I get to be as big as him?"

Finally putting her menu down, there's a glimmer of mischief in Sage's blue eyes, "I'm not entirely sure baby cakes, I don't think anyone could be as big as Dean."

You don't say?

The innuendo goes right over our girl's head, but I hear it loud and clear.

"You're probably right mom, I've never seen anyone as big as him."

Sage covers her mouth as she chuckles, blush turning darker, "Me either, sweets."

Grabbing a crayon from the children's menu, Jeri tunes us out and doodles all over the page. I slide my hand onto Sage's thigh under the table, rubbing circles on her warm flesh. Clearing her throat, she asks, "What sounds good to you?"

Pretending to read my own menu, I inch my hand higher under her sun dress. When I reach the seam of her panties, I drag my finger down and find a small wet patch on the front of the cotton. Stroking it lightly, I hear the slightest intake of breath. Sage slowly brings her hands down, grabbing my wrist, trying to halt my movements.

She's not successful.

As I keep stroking, I answer nonchalantly, "Honestly, everything sounds good. I'm starving."

When I look over, her face is flush, such a pretty red. Freckles almost blending in entirely. Her eyes have dilated, and that bottom lip I love so much is pulled between her teeth. I can tell she's stifling a moan. When she starts involuntarily rocking those hips against my hand, I stop, and her mouth pops open in protest, then she remembers we're in a restaurant and sits up straighter, refocusing on Jericho. I've decided working her up is too much fun. Later, when it's just the two of us, I want her ravenous. Then she can tell me if there's anything to worry about. Over the last eight years, I've never so much as touched another woman. Why would I want to now? She has no reason to be jealous, I plan to prove that to her.

We ate our meal as Jeri peppered me with questions, most of them I was happy to answer.

Did I like soccer? Yes, and I'd love to see her play.

How old am I? I'm 28.

Have I always been older than her mom? I laughed at that but answered yes.

Exactly how tall am I? 6'4".

When did I fall in love with the Songbird? When I was 13 years old.

Will I be staying for good? On this one, my eyes cut to Sage's. There was a hopeful expression on her face, but I could tell she was trying to hide it. Taking Sage's hand across the table, I turned back to Jericho.

"You see, that's something I've been meaning to talk to your mom about, I was offered a job here, so I could stay as long as you and your mom want me to."

Jeri looked at her mom's hand wrapped in mine, brows furrowed, then back up at me. "Are you going to take it? I think you should. My mom's been alone, and Tia Tess said it's not good for her. You're going to be good for her right?"

"I think your Tia is right, it isn't good for her, but when you think about it, she hasn't been alone, because she's had you. But I promise, I'll be good to your mom."

Eyeing me for a moment, she smiles, seemingly satisfied with my response. I can't answer being here for good, not wanting to promise anything, it's a conversation Sage and I need to have soon though. The thought of leaving them causes physical pain. The offer is there, I plan to take it once I know for sure where we stand. I've already missed so much time, I don't want to miss anymore. *Wherever they are, that's home.* I'm positive we can make it work.

Picking up a crayon, she doodles a bit more before asking, "Did you have anyone, or were you alone too?"

Sage squeezes my hand; I can feel the guilt emanating from her. Squeezing back, I answer her. "I wasn't always alone; my brothers and my father kept me company. But I did miss your mom very much and I think she probably missed me too.

Sometimes, when you can't see the one person you most you want to, it can feel lonely, even when you're surrounded by people."

The poker face on this girl could rival Jora's. Finally, she nods and finishes her food quietly.

When the waitress brings the bill, I insist on paying and then we head home.

Spending the day with the girls was amazing. Finally getting a glimpse into the life Sage has built for herself and our daughter, I'm so fucking thankful that she's the mother of our child. I hate that I missed so much, but from this point forward, I don't plan to miss a thing. This life, I want it. I've always wanted it. Things didn't go quite how they should have, but in the end, we're getting a second chance. My girls are dancing in the living room to some pop song while I sit back on the sofa and just watch. When Jeri sees me being too relaxed, she bounces over and tries to yank me off the couch. Her little arms make no headway, it's like watching her try to push a brick wall. Laughing, I heave myself up and twirl her around. The smile on this girl's face is the most beautiful thing I've ever seen. Her eyes are lit like diamonds and her dimples are on full display. Giggling, she twirls out of my spin and runs towards her bedroom when Sage tells her to go get pajamas on before we settle in for a movie. When the song switches to something slower, I wrap my arms around Sage from behind and we sway. Feeling the heat of her body and breathing in her lemongrass scent, I'm happy just soaking her in. Running her hands across my forearms, she relaxes into my hold.

"I love having you here Raven."

Leaning forward, I burrow my face into her neck. "I love being here Songbird."

Turning in my arms, she loops her own around my waist, palms pressed to my back, and we bask in the beauty of the moment. Jeri pops back into the living room, unicorn jammies on, with a blanket and no less than three plushies tucked under her arm. Sage presses a kiss to my chest and pulls from my embrace. When she goes to make some popcorn, Jeri and I pull throw pillows off the couch and pick a movie.

Settling on the sofa, Sage comes over and snuggles up with me. Jeri takes the pile of pillows and blankets on the floor and starts *'Tangled'.* I'm so unbelievably comfortable, it isn't long before I feel my eyes drift shut and I'm fast asleep.

Sometime later, fingers are running through my hair. When I crack my eyes open and start to lean forward, Sage holds her hand up, silencing me, then motions towards a sleeping Jericho on the floor. The girl is a mess of black curls and unicorns. Her mouth is hanging open, a bit of drool pooling at the corner, she's sleeping hard. Lifting from the sofa, Sage arms the security system and starts to lift Jeri from her sleep pile. Stopping her, I whisper, "Go get the bed ready, I'll take her."

Squatting down, I unwrap the baby burrito that is Jericho and lift her in my arms. Her weight is nothing to me. When I pull her to my chest, she sighs, and it almost does me in. I've felt nothing but content since the moment I saw her. This is something I never knew I needed, being a father.

Besides her mother, this girl in my arms is the most important person in my world. Walking into the bedroom, Sage is drawing back the comforter and fluffing her pillow. After laying her on the sheets, I crouch down and gaze at her sleeping face. Sage places a soft kiss on Jeri's forehead and runs fingers through her curls.

"She's beautiful, Songbird. The best parts of both of us." Placing her hand on my shoulder, she squeezes it briefly. Before she can pull away, I grab and kiss it. Standing, I don't let go of her hand as

I guide her towards the master bedroom.

When we arrived, I closed the door gently and took a moment to look at her.

This woman, this perfect soul. Now that she's here, I'm never letting her go. I won't survive it a second time. Never taking her eyes off mine, Sage starts to undress slowly.

When she's standing naked before me, baring all, I do the same. Each article of clothing falling to the floor is a countdown. Her blue eyes are glowing, and her skin is flush. When I finally pull my boxers off, she licks her lips and I zero in on the movement. I'm not sure who moves first, but I can't kiss her enough, can't touch her enough. My hands start on her face, travelling to her hair, then slide down her back. Grabbing her perfect ass, I lift her to me. Strong legs wrap around my waist, and pillowy lips move across my jaw, continuing a path down my neck. Without breaking contact, I walked us to the bed and laid her down gently.

Our previous couplings have been quick, emotionally charged. *Savage.*

But this, I want to make love to her. My arms come up beside her face, caging her in. Her eyes go from half lidded to wide open when I speak, "I love you, Sage. I've always loved you. You're the light, my beautiful Songbird."

Raising her fingers to my lips, she traces them, as if feeling the vibrations left behind by my words. Leaning up, she plants a small kiss to each corner of my mouth. Settling back into the pillow, her response is warbled, "I love you too Dean. I've always loved you. I always will."

I've said I didn't need a great proclamation, but this, having heard it, I didn't know I needed it. Every brick I've built around my heart comes crashing down just as my mouth does over hers. I kiss her passionately, swallowing her moans as she opens for me.

She tastes of popcorn, and I dive deeper, running my tongue over her teeth and sucking her bottom lip into my mouth. Moving from her lips to her jaw, to her neck, I traced a path down to her stomach and then between her thighs. At the first swipe of my tongue over her pussy, she arches and runs her fingers into my hair. Shoving my tongue inside her, I work it slowly, in and out before moving back to her clit and biting. With a quiet gasp, she starts to ride my face from below.

It gives me an idea.

Flipping us over, I pull her on top of me. With hands on her hips, I start to guide her to straddle my face, but she pauses, protesting. "Dean, no, I'm too heavy."

The fuck she is.

"Songbird, grab the headboard and sit on my face, if it's how I go, I'll die a happy man, drowning in your sweet pussy."

When she still doesn't move, I growl, "Get. Up. Here." Hesitantly, she starts to move, but it's not quick enough. Grabbing her hips, I put her right where I want her. Then I eat. Finally relaxing into me, she rides for real. Grinding her pubic bone into my nose, small gasps pop out when she finds her rhythm. *It's erotic and everything I want.* I could live off the taste of her. Like the sweetest honey running over my tongue. From back to front, I lick everywhere but her clit. When she starts to whine and shift her hips some more, I concede and pull her clit between my lips and nibble, rolling the little bundle of nerves between my teeth as I work my tongue back inside her. Letting all inhibitions go, she lets go of the headboard and brings her fist to my hair. Running my arms up her thighs, I dig my fingers in and pull her to me tighter. When that first orgasm hits, it's ecstasy, I lick every drop as it floods my tongue, *I'll never get enough of her.*

Lifting her off me, I roll us again and bring my mouth down to hers, "See how good you taste Songbird." Kissing her deeply, I position myself between her thighs and coax my fingers down her leg. Grabbing her knee, I pull it higher as I start rubbing my dick against her folds, back and forth, popping my crown in an out, driving her mad. When she can't take it anymore, she huffs, "Dean, stop teasing, I need you. I need you so badly."

Fighting a smile, I lean in close to her ear and whisper, "And I need you, don't you understand? Never doubt that." gesturing between us, "Baby you're all I want."

Grabbing her hands, I rest them beside her head, locking our fingers together. My arms are shaking with anticipation. But I promised to take my time. Slowly, I push into her tight cunt, inch by inch. She grips me so well, so warm and wet and perfect. When I'm seated to the hilt, she gasps, and I groan.

God this feels fucking incredible.

Resting my forehead on hers, I shift my hips and pull out slowly before repeating the action. In slow, measured thrusts, I can feel every inch of her coiled tight beneath me. While moving inside her, a sense of peace washes over me.

"Take it Songbird."

She gasps out, eyes wide, "I need to touch you."

"Patience baby." With that promise, I snap my hips harder, increasing the pace. Her back arches putting her tits right where I need them to suck a nipple into my mouth. Working one into a hard point and then moving onto the other. I plant sloppy kisses all over chest, biting and sucking, leaving my marks. Releasing one of her hands, I bring the other between her legs and rub her clit in time with my thrusts. She locks her ankles around me, and I pull back slightly to watch her perfect tits bounce as she unravels.

I've said it already, but it Does. Feel. Fucking. Incredible.

I wanted to take my time, but my plans need to change. This is so charged, I'm not sure how much longer I can hold out. With another pump, I pull up unto my knees and take her with me. She straddles my lap as I pull her back onto my dick.

"Dean."

"I know baby, be a good girl and ride me. Give me another one."

Hooking her arms around my neck, she slams her mouth onto mine, copper hair becomes a curtain around us. *My girl rides me so well.* Skin slapping skin echoes around the room like music. Slipping a hand up, I cup her breast and roll her nipple between my fingers, pinching and tugging. Her head falls back on a long moan, and I use the opportunity to lick a trail up her chest. With one more bounce on my cock, she comes.

Ohhhh how she comes.

Rippling walls almost undo me, before she has a chance to ride the wave completely, I push her back down, hooking her legs over my shoulders and slam into her *hard*, hips pounding erratically, chasing my own release. Coming with a roar, I keep going until she's taken *every last drop I give*.

Falling to my side, she rolls into me. Sex with her before? That was two fumbling teens getting it done as quickly as possible, because they were on limited time. Sex with her now? *It's mind blowing.* I'm covered with sweat, but she doesn't seem to care. Curling up on my chest, she strokes my tattoos lazily. Catching her hand, I bring her fingers to my lips, kissing them before setting it back down and covering it with my own. We stay just like that, when her breathing evens out, I couldn't move now even if I wanted to. With a lightness in my soul, I close my eyes and fall asleep with her.

CHAPTER TWENTY-TWO

Sage

The next morning, I reach across my bed, expecting to feel a large man, instead, my palm lands on cool sheets. Sitting up, I search the room and come up empty. I know he wouldn't just leave. Not after yesterday, not after last night. The rich smell of coffee wafts in through my cracked bedroom door, accompanied by Jericho's giggles. Rising from the mattress, I use the restroom and splash some water on my face before wrapping a robe around myself and following the sounds of laughter.

I stop short when I get to the end of the hallway, Jeri has one of my dining chairs pulled to the counter as she and Dean crack eggs. There's batter on her smiling face. Not noticing me yet, I creep closer and lean against the door frame. Jeri says something and Dean throws his back, filling the kitchen with the sound of his rich laughter. Something about seeing the two of them like this fills me with so much love, my heart could burst from it.

When Dean turns to pour their egg mixture into the skillet, he catches me spying and gives a small wink. Nudging Jeri with his elbow, he tilts his head in my direction. My girl bounces from her chair and grabs my hand pulling me into the kitchen with them as she prattles, "Mom, you're finally awake! The Raven said we should let you sleep. Did you have good dreams?"

Both dimples are on display, her unbridled joy warms me to my soul. Running my fingers over her face, I smile back. "I had a great sleep. Did you, sweets?"

She bounces excitedly, "Yes! When I woke up this morning, the Raven asked if I wanted to make pancakes. He said we should surprise you. Are you surprised mom? Are you?"

"I am so surprised! It was very thoughtful, and I can't wait to try some of your pancakes."

Clapping excitedly, she moves back towards her father. Dean stands at the stove, flipping pancakes and scrambling eggs. He looks fucking edible himself, in grey sweats and a white shirt that hugs his glorious chest and biceps, bumping him softly with my hip, I ask, "Did the Raven happen to make any coffee?"

He leans over and gives me a small peck on my cheek, "He did. There should be plenty left in the pot. Coffee is one of my staples."

Reaching into the cupboard, I grab my favorite 'mommin ain't easy' mug, "Mine too. I'd hook up an IV if I could."

When I make mine how I like it, I pick up his mug too noticing it's half empty. "Do you want some more?"

Helping Jeri plate food, he nods. "Yes, please. If you don't mind."

Noticing there's not discoloration I ask, "No creamer?"

He chuckles, "No creamer, but a spoonful of sugar would be great. If you don't care, take it to the table and we'll bring the food over."

My girl chimes in, "Yeah mom, go sit. We got this."

Hands raised in surrender, I do just that.

The breakfast is delicious, and the company is even better. Not able to eat another bite, I sip my coffee and watch the two of them interact. I'm not sure I've ever been this happy, I never want him to leave. There's a small part of my brain that's still worried about it, we made a life here, Jeri and I, Dean has a life in Ravenswood. How will we manage that? Will he expect us to leave? From the look on his face yesterday when Jeri was asking, I know it's something we need to address soon. His place is here. With us. At the restaurant, he mentioned a job offer. I'll need to dive deeper into that and see what it would mean for us. As the two of them finish up, I stand, starting the cleanup process.

"Hey Songbird, I can do that." Scooting his chair back, Dean goes to take the plate from my hand.

"No, it's okay. You two cooked for me, the least I can do is clean. Why don't you and Jeri go hang out for a bit? I'll give you some time before I come find you. I'm just going to do this and go shower."

At the mention of showering, his eyes heat before he shakes his head, clearing it away.

"Come on Raven, I want to show you my doodle book." With a peck on my forehead, Dean lets Jeri drag him to her room.

After cleaning the kitchen, I strip the sheets from my bed and throw them in the wash and pull a fresh set from the linen closet. Walking back into my room, I think of the burner phone, I haven't checked it in a few days. Pulling it from the dresser, it won't turn on. Remembering, when I shut it off a few nights ago, I never charged it. Correcting that mistake, I plugged it in and placed it in the drawer out of sight. I've not mentioned having it to Dean, I'll need to do that soon.

Once I finish making the bed, I jump in the shower and clean up quickly. After throwing on some comfy clothes, I go in search of Jeri and Dean. Making my way down the hall, I note they're not in her bedroom. When I hit the living room, I see that it's been cleaned from the night before. Throw blankets are folded and set on the sofa, but they're not in there either. Walking into the kitchen, I peer out into the back yard. Jeri has a soccer ball and the two of them are kicking it back and forth. Dean trips, whether intentionally I'm not sure, but when he falls, Jeri bursts with laughter and dog piles him. After a few moments of roughhousing and tickles, he holds his hands up shouting 'uncle'. She hops off him and skitters away, squealing, popping back up, he's hot on her heels as he tackles her softly into the grass. Watching them play, I don't want to intrude on this time. After all these years they need it. Deciding I could use some more coffee, I refill my cup as my phone pings. It's Tessa.

Tessa: What do?

That's her standard greeting, one that's rubbed off on me.

Harlow: Sipping coffee. What do?

Tessa: Nothing really, just finished a yoga session and decided to see how things were going with you and the baby daddy?

Sneaking towards the patio door, I discreetly snap a picture of them before sitting back at the dining table and send it to her. They've stopped wrestling and are sitting on the grass, talking as Jeri puts small braids in his hair.

Tessa: Aww Dios Mio! That's amazing friend. Are you spending the day together?

Harlow: I think so. He hasn't said any different.

Tessa: I'm so happy for you hermana. You and mi niña. I'll let you get back to it. Call me later, okay?

Harlow: Will do. Love you. *heart emoji*

Tessa: And I love you. *kisses emoji*

Curiosity gets the best of me, making my way back towards the patio, I pull open the glass door, leaving the screen in place. Bits and pieces of their conversation float towards me.

"Can I call you something different than Raven? What's your name?"

Dean picks pieces of grass, pulling them between his cupped thumbs. It looks like he's trying to show Jericho how to whistle with them. He motions for her to cup her hands, demonstrating with his own as he answers her, "My name is Dean Graham. But you can call me anything you want. Anything that makes you feel comfortable."

Jericho gapes at him, "Your last name is Graham?"

He looks at her, nodding slowly. "Yes. My last name is Graham."

Oh shit, I don't think that's a subject that's come up yet. When the agent was creating my new identity, I made a request, one that he said made me an idiot, but I didn't care. A request I hadn't thought to mention. Before I can stop her, Jericho reveals it. "My last name is Graham too."

A choking sound bubbles from my throat and Dean whips his head in my direction. Stepping outside, I start to explain nervously. "It never came up, I'm sorry. I just wanted to make sure she had her father's name."

His eyes are wide, like a deer in headlights. Moving towards the two of them cautiously, I'm afraid he's short circuited. Jeri puts her small hand on his arm, and he jolts, looking down at her before asking hoarsely, "What's your full name Jeri girl?"

Proudly, Jeri recites it, "My name is Jericho Bea Graham."

Clearing his throat, "Is that so?"

"Uh huh, yep, mom said I was named after my granny."

Looking from her to me, he asks softly, "You named her after my mother?"

"I did. I loved your mom. She was one of the strongest women I'd ever known. I wanted to honor her in some way," Biting my lip, I ask, "Are you mad?"

Wringing my hands, I wait for him to respond. His head cocks to the side as he considers what I've asked, it's hard to read him. Slowly, he shakes his head, a soft smile overtaking his beautiful face, "I'm not mad, I love that you did that, what is your full name now?"

Smiling bashfully, I lay it on him. "While I do go by Harlow, if this is your way of asking if my last name is Graham too, then you'll be happy to know, it is."

Mouth popping open, I watch as the breath stalls in his lungs. Dean clambers off the ground and lifts me in a crushing hug, voice thick with emotion as he rasps in my ear. "I can't tell you how happy it makes me that you share my name, but one of these days, we're going to make it real. You're going to be my wife, Sage." Pulling back, he sets me back on my feet.

"Is that so?"

Kissing me on the forehead softly, he murmurs against my skin, "Fuck yes, it is. When this is all over, you're going to be mine, permanently. I'm not going anywhere Songbird. I'm going to accept the position that's been offered to me. It was something I wanted to talk to you about." Stepping back, he grabs my hands and pulls me onto the grass with Jeri, looking between us, he takes a breath, "How would you feel if I stayed here, with you? With the both of you?"

Jericho's a ball of excitement, practically bouncing with joy, she looks at me hopefully. There's only one answer to give, with a serpentine smile, I do. "We're yours, I've just been waiting for you to catch up."

At that he barks out a laugh and pulls me in, kissing me for real. Jericho claps beside us, "Does this mean I can call you dad now?"

Making a low whine Dean pulls back from me so quickly, I'm

surprised he doesn't topple over. He pulls our daughter into his lap and looks down at her, so much love and admiration in his gaze. When he finally speaks, his voice is thick with emotion, and I can see unshed tears in his eyes. "I'd love it if you called me dad, nothing would make me happier. It's an honor Jericho Bea."

She giggles and throws her arms around his neck, hugging him tight. I can't think of a more perfect moment. Unable to contain myself, I wrap my arms around both of them. I'm still on cloud nine when Dean's phone goes off. He hugged Jeri to him one more time before fishing it out of his pocket, when looking down at the screen, a frown marred his brow.

Our perfect bubble is bursting. I can feel it.

"Girls, give me just a minute, I need to take this." Climbing to his feet, he steps into the house as the two of us remain in the grass. Jeri scooches into my lap, and we decide to lay back and watch the clouds.

A few minutes later, I turn my head as Dean walks back into the yard, fully clothed, cut covering a black t-shirt. Gesturing for me to come talk to him, I do. Jeri fell asleep in the grass; it's been a busy morning. Stepping in the kitchen, I don't move farther than the door, so I can see her. Dean's standing at the table pulling his hair back into a loose bun. I patiently wait for him to finish, when he does, the look on his face has my hackles rising. "What's wrong? What happened?"

Pulling out a chair for me, he does the same and we sit at the table.

I'm not liking this so far.

He leans forward, clasping his hands together on the table.

"Dean, talk to me."

Looking in my eyes, his face softens, "That was Jora, he's in town. So is my dad and your brother. They're waiting for me at the clubhouse. But that's not what I'm concerned about...they aren't the only ones waiting."

Taking his hands in mine, I ask, "Who has you concerned?"

Reaching forward, he tucks a stray strand of hair behind my ear and looks over my face, as if he's memorizing every detail. "Your father is with them. My Pops said a man in Pete's club informed him of the situation, informed him about you. I'm to go face the music so to speak.' He laughs dryly, "I'm not sure how it'll end up, but I have faith. Nothing is going to keep me from you and our daughter Sage. But I have to talk to the man."

"Do you want me to come with you?"

Shaking his head quickly, he buckles down, "No, it's going to be okay. I've got to go; they're waiting for me to start church. Just... Stay here baby, okay? See if Tess can come over, keep you girl's company. There are a few brothers around keeping an eye on your place. Let me put my number in your phone though, just in case."

Pulling my cell from my pocket, I hand it over. He calls himself and saves my number as well. Handing it back to me as he stands from the table, I follow him to the door. Before he walks out, he grabs my face and brings his mouth to mine. Kissing me softly at first, then harder. My hands come up to his chest and he slides his arms around me. Breaking it before I'm ready, he pulls away and strides for his bike.

As he fires it up, the straight pipes rumble loudly, Dean pulls his bucket helmet over his head and his baclava over his face. Backing out of my drive, he blows me a kiss before taking off.

Standing on my porch, I watch him get smaller and smaller before eventually turning out of view. Stepping back inside, I walk back to the yard and carry a sleeping Jericho into the house and focus on settling her in bed. She's had a busy week, and the last 24 hours have been eventful. Needing my best friend, I sent Tessa a text.

Harlow: Come over?

Her response comes quickly.

Tessa: I'll be there in 20.

CHAPTER TWENTY-THREE

Dean

Arriving at the Saints clubhouse, I park my bike at the cottage. Jora comes to greet me as I'm climbing off the Harley. Pulling me in for a one-armed hug, he clasps my back and takes me in, smiling. "Why Dean, you're practically glowing brother. Did you finally break your dry spell? Give the old handy a break?"

Rolling my eyes, I scoff at him, "Shut the fuck up J."

My father's voice booms from the cottage doorway, "Leave him be Jora. We've got to go. Glad you finally decided to show up son. They're waiting." Angus Graham brought his game face, the man who joked with me and Donnie on the phone is nowhere to be seen. Tucking his hands in his pockets, my father walks across the lot and towards the clubhouse proper. With a shrug, Jora clasps me on the shoulder and we follow. Whispering under his breath, Jora informs me that Donnie and Thorne are already in the meeting room and Colin's been holed up in Pete's office for the last couple hours. Just because the big man's here, doesn't mean he stops working.

Stepping into the clubhouse, the atmosphere is charged. You can tell the men are worried, the music is muted, and the conversation is stilted. Ignoring the looks directed our way, we stepped into the meeting room. Thorne sits across the room with Donnie, huddled together in quiet conversation. Shortly after we arrive, Petey does too. He doesn't take his seat at the head of the table, opting to leave it open for Colin.

Donnie looks up and notices me; while standing, he squeezes Thorne's shoulder before making his way over. The Raven's MC is displaying a united front. Jora moves closer to Thorne and takes his seat. My father sits to my right, and Donnie sits to my left. Our baby brother is noticeably absent, leaning into my father, I ask, "Where's Knox?"

"He'll be here tomorrow, there was something he had to pick up."

Satisfied, I lean back in my chair and wait, thinking about who I've got waiting for me at home. Picturing Jericho's smiling face, the way she asked to call me dad. I almost miss the thunderous footsteps approaching the room. Doors blast open and Colin finally storms through. He's an imposing figure. Standing at the head of the table, he doesn't sit, instead, he stands there, gripping the back of the chair as he takes in each face in attendance. Another set of footsteps and Jorge walks through, taking his position next to Colin.

The Don of the McGregor clan looks suave compared to Jorge. In his pressed black slacks and white button up, he's all class. When he sees everyone who should be here is present, Colin slowly starts to undo his tie and unbutton the top of his shirt. Without uttering a word, he begins rolling up his sleeves.

Finally breaking the intense silence, he drawls calmly, in a slight Irish brogue, "A wee little bird told me my daughter is alive. Anyone care to dispute that?"

Colin finally looks up at the men in the room. He looks so much like my Songbird, it's uncanny. Their blue eyes are the same shade, and his hair is copper too, just a bit darker. Clearing my throat, I held up a hand. "Sir, I can confirm she is indeed alive."

Pulling his pistol from behind his back, he slams it on the table, barking harshly, "Speak."

My father nudges me to stand, so I do. "Sir, your daughter is alive and well. We weren't aware of that fact until four days ago. She'd faked her own death to hide from the Medvedev Bratva."

Arching a brow, he rubs his hand over his jaw and smiles, though it's slightly deranged. "Why would she fake her death when she died 21 years ago lad?"

On that note, Thorne finally chimes in. "Sir, with all due respect, we weren't aware that she was your daughter until the incident Dean is speaking of."

"Ahhh, the 'law man', tell me boy, what do you know?" Thorne swallows before looking at me. "Don't feckin look at him! You look at me!" Colin roars, slamming his fist on the table.

Despite the outburst, Thorne replies evenly, "Sir, your daughter wasn't killed, she was placed in my mother's care when she was four years old, on the order of Vasily Medvedev. Being a child myself at the time, I had no knowledge of this until the incident eight years ago. Coming home for a visit, I was apprised of the situation by my mother, Hattie Bell Mason. My father was Clay Mason, a 'cleaner' for the Medvedev Bratva. When I found out, I reached out to the bureau and followed their instructions. My orders were to hide Sage by any means possible. I know it wasn't right, but I had a decision to make. For my career."

What the fuck Thorne?

At that, Colin grabs his gun and points it at Thorne. "Tell me why I shouldn't shoot you where you stand you pig fuck? Someone that blindly follows orders has no place here."

Unable to stop myself, I bark, "Wait." Colin levels me with a sadistic look, eyes bloodshot, never dropping his aim from Thorne. Despite the bottle resentment for the way he manipulated Sage into leaving, I can't let Colin kill him. It would hurt Sage. Time to drop the bomb. "If Thorne didn't do what he did, then your granddaughter wouldn't have been born."

That gives Colin pause, he lowers the gun slightly, eyes narrowed, trying to sniff out if I'm full of shit or not. Turning, his eyes find Jorge, the man gives him one imperceptible nod.

I knew I didn't fucking like that guy.

Snapping the gun back in the holster at his back, Colin instructs everyone to sit. He wants the story, the whole story.

So, Thorne and I comply.

Thorne starts by explaining how Sage came to be with them and about her childhood under his mother's care. He dives into her dreams, the nights she had to stay in his or his sister's rooms. Then the verbal and physical abuse Sage endured. As he talks, Colin's face grows redder and redder, his jaw clenches and his hand balls into a fist on the table. When Thorne gestures for me to take over, I do, without hesitation.

I'll never be sorry for loving Sage.

"Sir, I've loved your daughter since I was 13 years old." I told him about the time I heard her sing under the willow tree, "She was beautiful to me. Even though I wasn't sure what it meant, I loved her then, I love her now, I didn't touch a woman all the years I believed her gone, there was no one else, never will be." Blowing out a breath, I drop the other important fact, "Her daughter's name is Jericho Bea Graham, she's mine."

At that Colin's face goes from contemplative, to fucking *irate*.

When he goes to grab his gun, my father bellows, "Don't you *fucking dare* McGregor! You don't know everything yet. *Sit down*."

Clenching his jaw, he shocks the hell out of me by listening.

When he's a bit calmer, he narrows his eyes at my Pops, "I've said I don't want blind followers, I meant that. We've been friends for decades Angus, out of respect for you I will listen, but do not *ever*, and I *mean ever* forget that I am the Don."

My father scoffs, "I've not forgotten anything Colin, but you seemed to, this is my son. We protect our family, do we not? There's more the boy needs to say, you'd best listen."

Colin absorbs my father's words and motions for me to continue.

"As I was saying, Jericho is my daughter, but I wasn't aware of her existence until three days ago. I'm not going anywhere, sir. I will be with them from this point forward. I love your daughter, and she loves me. We'd always planned to have a family; this is just a roundabout way to get started."

Running the palm of his hand over the table, he crooks his fingers for Jorge to come forward. "I've had Jorge here since before Pete Sr.'s death. He's my man, always has been. I'm told that you're going to be taking over this charter, making it a Raven's club, that true?"

"Yes sir."

"You plan to do that and have my daughter by your side? Does she understand what you are, what you do?"

Fisting my hands under the table, I try to keep calm. Be the fixer I always have been. "She doesn't know all sir, but she knows enough."

"I could have Jorge running this place, he's loyal to me, capable. Tell me why I should let you take over instead of him."

Sitting up straighter in my chair, I stare into the Irish devil's eyes. "With all due respect to your man, he wouldn't do the job the way I can, anyone here can attest to that. This charter is in my blood, it flows through my veins. The discipline it would take, your man there doesn't have, he knows it too. Or he'd have stepped up when the change was voted on." Jorge shifts on his feet as I continue, "You want someone like me riding at your back, sir... if I'm being honest, this club will give my family the most protection."

He taps his finger on the table, "If my daughter asks you to give it up, what then?"

I don't hesitate, "I'll walk away, but she'd never do that."

Rubbing a hand along his lower lip, he asks, "Why not?"

Shrugging, I answer as honestly as I can, "It's who I am, it's one of the things she loves about me. She's not afraid of the darkness, not when she's the light."

Just then a shrill ringtone cuts through the room, everyone looks to the man next to them, but my eyes stop and catch on Thorne as all the blood drains from his face. He pulls a cell from his pocket and Colin barks at him, "Now isn't the time to be taking a bloody call lad, put that shite away."

Thorne ignores him, answering, "Sage, I'm kind of in a-"

Pulling out my phone, I don't have a missed call or text from her, why did she call her brother?

His breath catches and I can just make out her panicked voice over the line. She's shouting so loudly; I can hear her from across the room. I'm up before he is, charging over.

Thorne stands, eyes wild, looking at me, "Call an ambulance, we're coming. Stay on the line... Yeah, he's here."

He thrusts the phone in my direction and her anguished sobs pour out, "Sh-sh-she's, she's, she's gone. They took her, ohmygodtheytookher, they took my girl Dean!"

Donnie comes up beside me, pressing his ear closer, listening in. I've never felt fear greater than I do in this moment, "Baby, I'm coming, where are you?!"

"H-h-home, Dean please," Her voice takes on a hysterical edge, she's in a full-blown panic attack, "p-please, hurry. Tessa's hurt, s-she's hurt." I'm already on the move, Donnie whips his head in my direction. When he hears that, he storms from the room ahead of me, I don't wait for dismissal, I'm hot on his heels. "Stay on the phone baby, I'm coming." I holler at Donnie, "No bikes, grab a cage!"

The prospect in the garage tosses my brother a set of keys and we climb into the square body we'd previously borrowed, Donnie drives and I shut everything down, focusing on calming my girl.

One thing at a time.

"Baby, we're going to get her back, they're not going to hurt her, now I need you to focus, is Tessa breathing?"

Shuffling sounds from the line, "Y-y-yes. But barely. Oh my God. Dean. Please hurry."

Putting her on speaker, I texted the brother who was supposed to be watching her house, trying to figure out what the fuck happened. Donnie cuts in from the driver's seat, his voice unbelievably calm despite the way his knuckles are gripping the wheel, "Sage, you have a security system, right?"

She hiccups, "Yeah."

I take over, knowing where he's going with this, "Baby, can you get to your alarm panel? I don't want you to hang up, there should be an emergency button. If you push that, it'll send an ambulance to your address. Can you do that baby?"

"Y-yes, but Dean," her voice lowers to a whisper, "I've b-been, sh-shot."

No, no, no. Please, no.

"Baby, how bad is it, where were you shot?"

Sounds come through, like she's dragging herself, "My leg, m-my leg." She hisses before groaning out, "I got it, ambulance is being routed."

Not only is my girl having a panic attack, she's in shock.

"Songbird, I need you to try and stay calm, you're doing so well. I'm so proud of you. We're going to get Jericho and you're going to be alright." She's gone quiet, "Songbird, are you with me?"

Still nothing, fuck. FUCK. FUCK.

Slamming my fist on the dash, I snarl at Donnie, "GO FUCKING FASTER!"

He disregards all traffic laws and cuts through everyone, when we finally make it to Sage's house, two ambulances and several police cars are already there, one loading an unconscious Tessa who's on a stretcher. When Donnie makes it to her side, there's so much blood, she's soaked. A knife is sticking out of her stomach and the medics gloved hand stays on the hilt, stabilizing it. I'm positive the only reason she isn't dead yet is because it wasn't pulled out.

My brother loses his mind, muttering 'Wildcat' and his knees start to buckle. Catching him before he could, I instructed him to climb into the ambulance and go to the hospital with her. When the paramedics argue, he snarls at them, "I'm fucking going, try to stop me." Without further protest, he climbs on board.

Pushing past the crowd, I go into the house to find Sage being loaded up, she's unconscious as well. Her leggings have been cut to reveal a bullet wound in her thigh and her face is ghostly pale. When I enter the living room, they try to usher me away, but I'm not having it. "That woman is my wife, Harlow Graham, I'm Dean Graham."

A police officer blocks my path, he takes in my cut and eyes me with suspicion. "Sir, do you have any idea what happened here?"

Shaking my head, I glance around the living room. Furniture is toppled, books strewn all over the floor. There's blood, so much fucking blood. Ignoring his question for now, I march down the hallway into Jericho's room. Her room isn't as trashed, but I can clearly see there was a struggle. Her rug is folded back, like she was dragged from under her bed. The terror she must have felt, grasping my chest, I made my way back to Sage. I have to lock it down. If Mihailo has Jericho, he's not going to hurt her. The fact I've never known him to hurt children doesn't ease the fear entirely, but it helps. I can't leave until I know Sage is going to make it. The police officer is still in the living room when I storm back through, when I move to the door, he blocks my path again, "I have no idea what happened, but I'm going to the hospital with my wife. Move or I will move you." I snarl coldly, "If you have questions, come find us there."

With that, he nods nervously and lets me pass.

Someone hurt my Songbird and took my daughter.

They fucked up, I'll burn everything down to find her.

CHAPTER TWENTY-FOUR

Sage

ONE HOUR EARLIER

Tessa showed up with a plethora of foods, knowing the way to my heart. Setting everything up in the kitchen we fixed plates of tamales and birria tacos before moving into the living room to listen in case Jeri wakes up from her nap. Groaning at all the deliciousness, I inhaled my food. Taco halfway to her mouth, I caught Tessa staring at me.

"What? Do I have something on my face?" Wiping my cheeks, I took in her incredulous expression.

"No mami, you're inhaling your food. Burn a lot of calories recently, did you?"

Rolling my eyes, I pick up my water and sip, "I'm hungry. That's all. You always make the best food."

Clucking her tongue, she takes a bite and mulls over my paltry excuse. When she finishes chewing, she wipes her fingers daintily with a paper towel and smirks at me. "I told you I'd find out all your secrets... was it good?"

Just thinking about her question has my cheeks flaming and my vagina clenching. Opening my mouth, intending to tell her nothing, I do the opposite, I word vomit. "It was so fucking good, like, earth shattering, soul sucking, good."

Cackling, she rushes across the sofa to me. "I knew it! I told you he had the energy! You finally got your oil changed and I couldn't be prouder! Did you climb that man like a tree? I need information, I'm living vicariously through you."

"Vicariously, what do you mean?" I laugh loudly, "You're no saint Tess."

Sighing dramatically, my friend looks away before turning back. "I've been in a dry spell myself; I don't know what's wrong with me, but I'm tired of meaningless sex. I mean, yeah, it was great at first, but now, I don't know. Plus, with the bar growing busier, I don't have the time, and you *know* I don't sleep with patrons. Too messy, mixing business with pleasure."

Taking another bite of my taco, I hesitate to ask, but I've got to know, "What's going on with you and Donnie?"

It's her turn to blush, and Tessalynn Sanchez is *not* a blusher. When she doesn't reply, I gasp, "You like him? Don't you? You like the man."

She scoffs full of indignation, "I do not! I mean, okay, he's cute and funny and Dios Mio, *that body...* It's drool worthy, capital Y, yummy. But the man says he's going to marry me Harlow! MARRY. ME. Who says that to someone they've just met? To quote the greatest queen alive, 'You can't marry a man you just met'."

"You've been watching entirely too many movies with Jericho."

She wags her finger at me, appalled. "You can never watch too many *Disney* movies. How do you think I learned English?"

Blinking at her, I ask, "How you learned English?"

Nodding, "Yes, I watched *Disney* movies. I know every princesa there is."

Teasingly I ask, "Are you telling me you're a *Disney* fanatic?"

"If you tell anyone that, I will cut you. I know how to skin someone properly, don't make me prove it."

Laughing loudly, "You're telling me you're a *Disney* fanatic and that you know how to properly skin someone in the same breath? Who are you?"

At that, the blood drains from her face. I know Tessa has her own demons, and while we've talked about some of them, I didn't know the whole story. If I've unwittingly triggered her, I didn't mean it. Clasping her hand in mine, I apologize. "Hey, I'm sorry, that was just me teasing. Who you were doesn't matter to me, only who you are now."

She grimaces at me, "I know hermana, there's just a lot you don't know about and I'm afraid once you do, you won't want anything to do with me."

Shaking my head, I tell her sternly, "There isn't a single thing about you that could scare me away, my friendship doesn't come with stipulations. That's not the way this works. You're my sister Tess, point blank. You're the fiercest woman I've ever known, and Jericho and I are damn lucky to have you in our lives, we're lucky that you have our back. No matter who you were or things you've done, I'm not going anywhere. I mean, Jericho's dad is an MC Vice President for fucks sake. He's a 1% club member. So is Donnie for that matter."

Gaping at me, she narrows her brows, "You mean, they're bikers? Like for real? Like... Mafia?"

"They are."

Her face pales and her lips quivers, before I have a chance to figure out why that would scare her, a knock sounds at my door.

I'd ignore it, but she turns her face so I can't see the tears pooling in her caramel eyes. Waving me away, she says, "Go get that, I'm okay. Give me just a sec."

Hesitantly, I stand, "Alright. Just know, I'm here. Always."

With that, I head to the door just as the knock sounds again, this time harsher.

Opening the front door, I see Brad standing on my porch and I'm concerned. "What are you doing here? I thought camp didn't get out until tomorrow? Is June okay?"

He smiles at me, but it's different than usual, stiff. "She's fine. Her mom is picking her up from camp, it's time for them to go back for the school year. I took off a day early, had some business to take care of. Do you mind if I come in, there's something I needed to discuss with you."

The vibes he's giving are making me hesitate, he's off. Somethings not right. It could be that he's upset about his summer visitation ending, maybe I'm reading too much into it. Stepping aside, I invite him in, "Sure, yeah, Tessa's here. Is this something that needs privacy?"

Shaking his head, he crosses the threshold, "No, it's fine. Won't take long."

When we step back into the living area, Tessa's face is clear, as if she was never upset to begin with. She purrs from her position on the sofa, "Hola coach Brad. How are you?"

He smiles at her, but it's still not reaching his eyes. "I'm well. And you Tess?"

She smiles back coyly, "I'm fine as can be, just catching up with my bestie here."

Ignoring her, I turn back to Brad, "You said you had something to talk to me about, what's up?"

Instead of answering me, Brad walks around my living room, taking in the books on my shelf and running his fingers across their spines. He speaks at the books when he answers me, "I wanted to talk to you about Jericho's dad actually."

"Why?"

Shrugging, he still doesn't look at me as he tilts his head up to look at an old photo I've recently put out. The box I pulled from the storage shed was full of them. Running his fingers across Jeri's face, he turns and looks over his shoulder at me. "He's not a good man, but you already knew that... didn't you Sage?"

"I'm not sure it's any of your business."

He ticks his finger up, "Ahh you see, it actually is my business, Sage."

At first, my brain didn't compute that he's just said my name. I've heard it so many times in the last few days, the change up from Brad doesn't register, but second time does it for me. My mouth gapes and I whip my head in Tessa's direction. She's sitting up straighter on the couch, the expression on her face murderous. "Hombre, you need to leave."

Clucking his tongue, he finally turns around and gives me a triumphant grin. Cocking his head in Tessa's direction, "You know what I find interesting? That a cartel princess is here at all. Does your father know you've wandered this far into the US? Started a business for yourself? How did you manage to accomplish that?"

At Tessa's gasp, I go to the door, holding it open, mustering all the hard ass I can, "You need to leave Brad. Now."

He laughs, shaking his head, still not moving, he carries on. "You know, I thought this would be a simple assignment, get close to you, find out what I could, maybe get a few good fucks out of it... They'd been suspicious for a while that you were who they were looking for. But they weren't sure. Not with you having a kid and all. I couldn't confirm until you brought the biker to pick up Jericho. You're her aren't you? Colin's daughter?" he laughs again, "I liked you, truly, but this isn't going to end the way you're thinking it will. I'm not going anywhere at all." Pulling a pistol from under his shirt, he levels it at Tess.

She growls at him and starts shouting in Spanish. "Estúpido hijo de puta. No tienes las pelotas para dispararme!"

Then a voice I haven't heard in years sounds from the doorway, the door I'm still holding wide open. The silky tones hit me right in the chest, "He might not, but I do."

Hattie Mason walks into my living room, I practically invited her in.

She smirks as she passes me. Just then, Jericho stumbles into the living room, wiping sleep from her eyes. "Momma, are you okay? I heard yelling."

I don't have time to panic, I push past Hattie and go towards her. But Brad beats me to it, he hides his gun behind his back and steps in front of her. Grabbing her by the shoulder, he squats down, "Hey Jeriberri," quickly turning back into the fun Coach B. "why don't you go back to your room for a little bit. Your mom and me need to have a grown-up talk."

Looking around him, her brows furrow, she can tell something is wrong. Nodding slowly, she asks, "Momma, will you come with me?"

Just then, Hattie saunters up beside me, the barrel of a gun presses into my back, and I stiffen. I can't do anything stupid, not with Jericho in the mix. As calmly as I can, I tell her smiling, "You go ahead baby. I'll be there in just a minute, promise."

From the corner of my eye, I catch Tessa slowly working her hand towards her ankle before tearing my gaze away and looking at my daughter. She nods again, still unsure, but finally goes back towards her room.

When she's out of shot, I whisper harshly, "What do you want?"

Hattie speaks conversationally beside me, "I want you to hurt. You've taken everything from me, so I'm going to return the favor."

Just then, Tessa lunges from the sofa and everything happens at once. Throwing herself at Brad, they slam into the bookshelf. Somehow, she has a small blade in her grip, slashing at his face. Caught unaware, she manages to cut down his cheek and blood pours. Popping an elbow up, he smashes her in the forehead. Disoriented, she stumbles, finally snapping back into myself, I charged past Hattie with a shove and ran towards them. That's when the gun goes off. One loud blast in the air and a burning heat flows through my leg, but I don't stop, there's too much adrenaline running through me. Grabbing Tessa off him, I go to push her behind me, but my leg trembles and caves. Wrenching me back by my hair, Brad throws me to the side and my back slams into my coffee table. He snatches the knife off the floor. I watch as Tessa screams and charges him again, that's when he rears back, shoving the blade into her stomach.

My world stops.

Both her hands came up slowly. Looking at me, she chokes out a whimper and falls. Looking around, I noticed Hattie's not in the living room anymore. Jeri screams from her bedroom and I muster up the last dregs of adrenaline to go to her. As soon as I lift myself from the floor, Brad spits on Tessa's body and moves towards me. I'm not quick enough before he's hooking an arm around my throat, bringing me back down.

From the hallway, Hattie drags a kicking and screaming Jericho into my line of sight.

No. No. No. No.

Jeri screams again, "Mommy!!"

Hattie places her hand over my girl's mouth and Jeri bites down. Before I can stop it, Hattie screams and rears back, hitting her over the back of the head, my girl's little body goes limp.

With that, I unleash. Twisting and fighting to get to my daughter. Brad tightens his headlock. Pushing my throat further into the arm in front of me. With Brad's arm around my neck, it's hard to speak. I snarl at her and thrash in his arms. "Let. Her. Go."

Brad's grip is crushing, black spots dance across my vision.

She continues to hold Jeri like a sack of potatoes, her curls dragging across the ground. Pointing her pistol at me, voice full of venom, she speaks. "I don't think so. This could have gone differently, you've only yourself to blame. Let McGregor know we'll be in touch."

With that parting remark, she carries my girl away. I kick and fight, but the angle Brad's got me in makes it hard. There's so much blood on the ground, my feet slip and slide, never finding purchase. And my leg, my fucking leg is burning with menace now.

Instead of trying to pull his arms from my throat, I say fuck breathing. As he squeezes again, I'm reaching up, running my fingers down his face, finally catching him with my nails and he shoves me away. "Bitch!"

Trying to catch my breath, I scream hoarsely, "How could you? She's only a child!"

He gathers himself up, gun aimed at Tessa. When I look over, she's still breathing, but it's shallow. "Don't do anything stupid, or I'll finish what I started. Cartel princess or not."

Walking to the kitchen, he dumps the contents of Tessa's purse onto the floor, finding her cell, he smashes it with the heel of his shoe. Then grabs mine off the counter, giving it the same treatment.

Crawling to her, I try to stop the bleeding, there's already so much. Her shirt is soaked as it pools on her abdomen and runs from the corner of her mouth.

She's going to die.

When I look back, Brad's gone.

It can't end like this, I can't.

What do I do?

I need to call someone.

Running my shaking hands through my hair, I try to think. That's when I remember, my burner cell is still in my nightstand.

Lifting myself from the floor, I use the walls, smearing blood as I go and make my way as quickly as possible. My injured leg is dragging behind me, the pain is beyond excruciating. Ripping the cell from my drawer, I power it on and make my way back to Tessa. Grabbing a throw blanket off the couch, I pressed it over her abdomen. My first call should have been 911, but I call my brother instead, someone needs to know in case I pass out from the pain.

Panic is setting in and I'm hyperventilating but I try to fight past it.

"Come on, come on, come on."

Finally, he answers. "Sage, I'm kind of in a-"

I scream, "NO! I don't care! Jeri is gone! They took her! I need help! Tessa's bleeding, my god Thorne, there's so much blood, she's going to die! They took my girl, I need you! I need Dean! Where is he, WHERE IS HE? Please, please, please! I'M TELLING YOU THEY TOOK JERICHO!"

CHAPTER TWENTY-FIVE
Sage

The sound of beeping wakes me from a dreamless sleep and the smell of antiseptic fills my nose. It's not hard to figure out I'm in a hospital. Fluttering my ashes, I try to force myself awake. I'm so tired, but there's no time for sleep, not when my daughter's been taken. Not when Tessa could be dead. Recalling what happened, my heart rate monitor starts going crazy. As I struggle to rise from the bed, a pain shoots through my thigh, and I cry out. Gritting my teeth with determination, I pat myself down, feeling all the lines connected to me. When I start to pull them off, a large hand closes over mine, startled, I rip my arm away and finally look at who's touching me.

For a moment, I'm taken back to a memory. Those eyes, like a cloudless sky. The same ones I see when I look in a mirror. I remember them and the feelings of peace they inspired. Right now, there's no peace to be found. He's trying to stop me and that just won't do. Snapping out of my haze, I start in on the IV ports again and pull the sticky heart monitors off my chest.

My throat is tender, and my voice comes out a raspy snarl, "Move."

Bristling in his Tom Ford suit, I can tell he's not used to people speaking to him the way I just have. His impatience quickly turns to concern, brows furrow as he takes in my face. Blue eyes bouncing back and forth before his face softens and he places his hand back on mine gently. The warmth of his palm is comforting despite how I feel. I know what those hands are capable of. I've done my research on the Devil of Chicago. There's so much blood on him, I'm surprised he's been able to wash it all clean. With a desperate plea, he whispers. "Mo chroí, no."

It's more vulnerability than I figure a man like him is capable of. He has a slight Irish accent, if I had to guess, I'd say it's been watered down over the years. I remember the pet name, the affectionate way he says it makes me shiver with repressed emotions. All the breath empties from my lungs and I'm involuntarily letting go of the IV at his whispered command. Unable to meet his eyes any longer, I looked around the room. I can tell it's expensive, private. To my left is a wall of floor to ceiling windows, the thick curtains are pulled closed. Making it hard to tell if it's night or day, hard to gauge how long exactly my daughter's been gone.

Finally sweeping my gaze back to him, I ask, "Have you found Jericho?"

Grabbing a chair, he pulls it to the edge of my bed. Unbuttoning his suit jacket, he sits, crossing one leg over his knee.

"No lass, we haven't. But we're looking."

"Who's looking?"

"Everyone."

It should make me feel better, but it doesn't. Until she's back in my arms, the band around my chest is only going to grow tighter. Trying to push back some of the anxiety, I ask a question I already know the answer to. "You're Colin, aren't you?"

"Aye lass, I'm Colin McGregor, do you know who you are?"

Laying my head back against the pillow, I answer. "I've heard things. But I'm not entirely sure if they're true."

He pulls his phone from his suit jacket pocket and taps it on his leg a few times.

"I'd know your face anywhere. It's your mother's, my Nora's."

"Nora?"

Nodding he lifts is phone and shows me images of a blonde woman, "Your ma."

She's beautiful. She has the same cupids bow I do, her cheek bones are high on her heart shaped face and there's the same smattering of freckles across her nose, matching my own and Jericho's.

Thinking of her only reminds me of the fact Jericho's been separated from me.

Panic sets back in. "How long have I been here?"

Standing from his chair, Colin makes his way to the window, pulling the curtains open. It's either sunrise or sunset, the golden rays shine through the room making it hard to know for sure.

"You got here yesterday afternoon, it's almost 8pm. They wheeled you into surgery upon your arrival and took the bullet out of your thigh. Luckily, it missed any major arteries. But I suspect you're going to be in a great deal of pain for a while. Gunshots are nasty business, I would know." Hands behind his back, he presses on. "We're going to find your daughter Mo chroí. Don't fret about that. My people are on it and that man of yours is too. Soon as he heard you were stable, he took off, mobilized his men. You've got bikers scouring every inch of this city as we speak. Smartest thing you can do is rest now."

"I can't rest. Not while she's out there."

He nods his head in understanding, "Aye, probably not. But I need to tell ya a story, best stay where you are for now."

While his tone is soft, I can feel the undercurrent of demand in it. His request is nonnegotiable. "A story?"

"Aye, lass."

Moving across the room, he sits back in his chair beside me and levels those piercing blues on my face. I know next to nothing about this man, but deep in my soul, I trust him. When he opens his mouth again, I listen.

"Your ma was a beautiful woman, which you've gathered, I'm sure. I fell in love with her during our first conversation. It wasn't just her beauty, she was enchanting. Captivating. The aura that Nora had, well, she did her name justice. She was light, pure light. And she was smart, so much smarter than me." He chuckles sadly, "Your ma, she saw the best in everyone. That was a lot of her appeal, but also her downfall. You see, Vasily Medvedev was a friend, we'd worked out an alliance years prior. All business coming through Chicago was either handled by me or him. I ran the Southside; Vasily handled the North. Several years of this went by and I could tell Vasily was itching for something different, he wanted to get into the skin trade. That's never something I've been alright with. I don't peddle in women and children. We had a fight, and he went off the rails. I wasn't aware at the time, but he'd started sampling the products we were selling. He'd get high, then go to a club and cause chaos."

Running his thumb and pointer finger across his temple, he paused for just a moment, collecting his thoughts.

"When he shot a man in front of a crowd of witnesses, that was it for me. I lashed out at him and things between us were stilted. My wife, my wonderful Nora, well, she didn't want tension, she was a fixer, that she was. Our families were already so tied together, and you'd been promised to Vasily's eldest son. So, she went over there one afternoon to talk to his wife -only, Natalya wasn't home- Vasily was." His hand drops from his temple and balls into a tight fist. Through clenched teeth, he tells me the rest. "Vasily brutalized your ma, my wife. He beat her, then he *raped her,* the man sent her back to me bloody and broken. It was then that I declared war, sending all of Chicago into an upheaval. A few months after, we find out Nora's pregnant. By this point, the war's in full swing. I've left a trail of bodies and burned down several businesses. But when I find out Nora's pregnant, and we're not sure if it's mine or Vasily's that's when I went nuclear. I killed someone I shouldn't have, someone my men respected. It gave Vasily an opening to turn a handful of them against me. He worked slowly, planted seeds of discord, promising money if they could help get rid of me. Called my wife a whore, claimed she'd come to him willingly."

Tears slowly track down my cheeks, bringing a hand up, I swipe them away and listen to the rest.

"Nora was eight months pregnant when they bombed the house. The two of you went missing and I was injured in the initial blast. I'm not sure what happened after I blacked out, but when I woke, you and your ma were gone. Angus Graham got me out and a month later, I'd moved to another safe house, continuing my search while healing. One afternoon, your ma's body was left at the end of the gate, her womb had been cut open and her throat slit. My beautiful Nora. Gone. Just like that. My daughter, my beautiful Saoirse missing, just like that. The unborn baby, gone." Finally, his voice breaks, he rasps the last bit. "Just. Like. That."

I've been riveted, listening to his tale this entire time. I'm not sure if telling him about my dreams will help, regardless, he deserves to know. "I cut my feet, after the blast." At that he stills, unnaturally so. But I press on, "We were running. There was glass on the floor and a man was with us, he picked me up. Then, we were in a car. Or an SUV maybe, it's the last thing I remember."

Leaning forward in his chair, he grabs my hand in his much larger one. Tilting his head, he stares at me with wonder. "You remember the fire?"

Nodding, my voice trembles. "I remember running. So much running. And she... she kept saying we 'had to make it to the safe house', that 'he could never find her', but I don't know who she was talking about."

"You lass, she was talking about you."

Rearing back my head, I ask, "Me? Why would she be talking about me?"

"Your ma was protecting you. The bombing was twofold. They were trying to take me out and get you. With the marriage contract signed, if Vasily had you, he could marry you off to his heir when you were of age and have a legitimate hold over the Irish Brotherhood. Seems like after Vasily's death, that was still their plan, it's why they kept you hidden with that awful woman."

In confusion, I ask, "Then why take Jericho?"

"I don't have an answer lass."

My eyes bounce back and forth between his, trying to piece everything together. The door to my room opens and someone I'd almost forgotten waltzes in.

A head full of chestnut hair, sapphire blue eyes and a cocky grin aimed in my direction.

"I think I can help with that."

Before I can ask what he's doing here, Colin snarls.

"Mihailo."

ACKNOWLEDGEMENTS

I'd like to start off by saying thank you to my incredible friend/ tattoo artist Whitney Taylor for the amazing cover design. I had an image in mind, and you brought it to life. Also, to Amy, my beta reader. Without your unfaltering support, this story may not have taken shape the way it did! I'd also like to thank my husband, Kerry. You've been a rock through this entire process, and I love you ever so much, thank you for being my Raven.

Fun fact, this story took shape in my mind and after two weeks of writing, I wasn't happy with the direction. Me being who I am, I teetered on what to do and agonized over it for days. Finally, I made the decision to scrap it entirely and went in a totally new direction. Once that choice was made, the words flew, and I couldn't have been happier. I've had so much fun writing this book and creating these characters!

Stay tuned, I can't wait to take you on the rest of the journey! Xoxo, E.